CHINT	GSHEL	ROCK
NKTRD	MILL	SAWST
LINT	FULB	WATG
BOTT	BURW	CSMJG 9/95

A Killing To Hide

Detective Chief Inspector Dick Tansey of the Thames Valley Police Force has married his erstwhile sergeant, Hilary, and the couple are delighted at the prospect of their first child. Tansey is therefore less than ecstatic when he is told that, as part of an official exchange programme, they are to leave the relative peace of their home patch while he spends six months in the more violent hassle of Central London, attached to the Metropolitan Police, with its reputation for arrogance and inflexibility.

On his arrival in Delta Mike Division, he finds himself immediately embroiled in one of the most intriguing and puzzling cases of his career. What is more, circumstances and staff shortages mean that he remains in charge of the inquiry, under the cynical eyes of the media, and with the assistance of a new detective-sergeant—Sester, a street-wise Met officer of some character.

As one apparently motiveless killing follows another, Tansey and Sester face a curious selection of suspects, mostly centred in the Marylebone area, and the Chief Inspector is forced to rethink his theories many times before the dramatic and unexpected climax.

JOHN PENN

A Killing To Hide

COLLINS, 8 GRAFTON STREET, LONDON W1

William Collins Sons & Co. Ltd
London · Glasgow · Sydney · Auckland
Toronto · Johannesburg

This book is fiction. All the characters and
incidents in it are entirely imaginary.

First published 1990
© John Penn 1990

British Library Cataloguing in Publication Data

Penn, John
    A killing to hide.—(Crime Club)
    I. Title
    823′.914[F]

    ISBN 0-00-232271-4

Photoset in Linotron Baskerville by
Rowland Phototypesetting Ltd
Bury St Edmunds, Suffolk
Printed in Great Britain by
William Collins Sons & Co. Ltd, Glasgow

CHAPTER 1

'Not exactly home from home, is it?' said Detective Chief Inspector Dick Tansey as he looked around the living-room. 'D'you think we can survive here for six months, darling?'

'Of course we can.' His wife made herself sound more cheerful than she felt. 'After all, it *is* only six months, and this is central London—and that's exciting enough in all conscience. I don't intend to spend my entire time shut up in this flat while you're busy being a shining example to the Met. Mind you, it may be a bit more difficult later on, but the baby's not expected till after we get back home.'

Thank goodness, thought Tansey, though all the right arrangements had been made for the care of his wife during their time in London. 'We'll both be pretty busy while we're here.' Tansey pulled her towards him, and kissed her on the mouth. 'And as you say, it is only six months,' he repeated, more to reassure himself than her.

'Oh, stop worrying, Dick. We'll be all right—certainly for such a short time,' Hilary said.

But Tansey was anxious. Until recently Hilary had been an efficient, hard-working detective-sergeant in the Thames Valley Police Force. Now the situation had changed completely. They had been married for only a short time before Hilary, to their joy, had become pregnant. Almost at once she had begun to suffer severe bouts of morning sickness, so that work had temporarily become impossible for her. She had soon largely recovered, but had decided not to resume her police duties. She still had had much to occupy her, however, apart from preparations for the baby—a search for a larger house with a larger garden than the one

Tansey already owned, for instance. And, though she and
Dick Tansey had been lovers for some while, marriage was
a new and unfamiliar relationship.

Then had come the bombshell. One morning Tansey had
been summoned to the office of Philip Midvale, the Chief
Constable, and had marched along the corridors of the
Kidlington Headquarters of the Thames Valley Force with
no suspicion of what was about to be asked of him. Only
when Midvale seemed to have difficulty in coming to the
point did he begin to feel any apprehension, though he still
had no reason to expect bad news.

'Tansey, the Home Office is very eager to demonstrate
that there is increasing cooperation and understanding between the various police forces in the country,' said the
Chief Constable at length. 'It seems to them that the alternative might be a national force, and that could well be
politically unpalatable. As you know, officers have often
been seconded to the Met, but usually only for training in
one or other of their special units—the Fraud Squad, the
Central Drugs Squad and the Criminal Intelligence Branch,
for instance. What is now intended as an experiment is that
officers should be interchanged between forces across the
country with other officers of like rank, age and ability,
actually to work, rather than merely train, for periods of
several months.'

'Yes, sir,' said Tansey automatically. Later he was to tell
Hilary that he must have been singularly stupid, because
at that moment he still had no idea of the direction in which
the Chief Constable was heading.

'Naturally, it's not easy to find suitable pairings,' Midvale
went on. 'Most, if not all, forces are under strength. Nobody
wants to spare one of their key men. But on the other hand,
honour forbids that we should send the Met a dud.'

'The Met?'

'Yes. The Thames Valley Force is to take part in the

experiment, and interchange with the Met to start with. It's already been arranged that a Detective Chief Inspector Porter is going to join us here for six months—and you, Tansey, will be taking his place in London, I hope. I'm sure you'll do us proud there.'

'But, sir!' The Met, which had a reputation for arrogance, rigidity and intractability, was the last force Tansey would have chosen, even for a temporary secondment. 'Sir, I hope you don't mean it,' he ventured at last. 'I'm perfectly content here, and there are innumerable reasons why it would be difficult, if not impossible, for me to move at present. My wife's expecting a baby, as you know, sir, and—and we're in the middle of house-hunting and—'

Tansey had enumerated his problems, knowing that they must seem increasingly trivial, though the Chief Constable had listened politely. Philip Midvale, a heavily-built man with an astute mind, was good at listening. But he had easily demolished Tansey's objections. London was expensive, undoubtedly, but there would be a generous weighting allowance, as it was called. Sergeant Greenway—Mrs Tansey—would have her maternity leave extended to fit the circumstances, and any necessary arrangements would be made for her care.

What was more, if the Chief Inspector did well, it would be a feather in his cap, and a big step towards promotion. Accommodation was no problem; if the Tanseys were pre-pared to let the Porters have their house in Kidlington, he and Hilary could have the use of the Porter's flat in Marylebone—bright, airy and close to Regent's Park, but within walking distance of the Police Station on Seymour Street to which Tansey was likely to be attached.

Now, at last in London, Tansey was groaning. 'The Chief's a con man,' he said, 'and so's that fellow Porter. How did I let them sell me on this dump, Hilary? It's small and dark, and as for being close to Regent's Park, there isn't

a tree in sight. I should have insisted on seeing it when I
was here for that week of briefings.'

'Cheer up, Dick. You couldn't insist—not if the Porters
had a sick child on their hands. Anyway, the Park's only a
walk up the road, and I suspect that on a sunny day the
whole place will look quite different. Besides, we haven't
bought it; it's only for six months,' Hilary said again consol-
ingly. 'Come on, love, let's get to grips with the rest of it.'

There was not a great deal more to inspect. The flat
consisted of an entrance hall about fifteen feet long, and
wide enough to contain a dining table and four chairs; it
was windowless, but the lighting had been carefully de-
signed and the hall was not unattractive. Four doors, two
on each side, led from it.

The first on the left opened on to the living-room where
the Tanseys were standing. It was well-proportioned, and
as the flat was on the first floor it had long Regency windows
stretching from the ceiling to low, upholstered window-
seats. The windows faced similar houses on the other side
of a fairly wide street. As Hilary had said, on a fine day it
would be full of light, though the Porters' colour scheme of
a bilious green and gold was not appealing.

Unfortunately the same colours continued into the bedroom next door. This was of a similar size and shape as the
living-room, with twin beds and built-in furniture. Hilary
wrinkled her nose in distaste at the sight of the cot in
which the Porters' two-year-old daughter had slept, and the
pushchair standing in the corner. She didn't want either of
them for her child, if by any chance it arrived early.

'What else?' said Dick Tansey. 'Presumably bathroom
and kitchen.'

These were on the other side of the hall, two narrow slits
of rooms, with small, high windows overlooking the backs
of other flats. There was no washing-machine in the kitchen,
Hilary noticed, and she thought of the chore of carrying

bed-linen along to a local washeteria. But otherwise the place was well-equipped. The Porters had left generous supplies of basic foods in the cupboards and fridge-freezer, and everything was spotlessly clean.

Suddenly Tansey gripped her by the shoulders. 'Hilary, are you sure you can be reasonably happy here? Because, if not—I'll be working damned hard, you know, and—'

'Darling—'

She was aware of why he needed to be reassured. When his first wife had walked out on him, taking their baby daughter with her, he had been philosophical about the predicament. Luckily his ex-wife had remarried and her new husband, a rich man, had been happy to adopt the child. For his part, Tansey had concentrated on his career. But this kind of trauma couldn't happen again. He was not prepared to let the exigencies of his life as a police officer ruin his second marriage. And yet he loved his work.

'Sir,' she said, drawing herself up to attention, 'you seem to forget you're addressing Detective-Sergeant Hilary Greenway—albeit on half-pay—who is quite aware of a policeman's lot and its problems—and who loves her husband very much.'

Tansey grinned, wondering how he had once thought that the composed and distant manner of this attractive dark-haired girl with her wide-set green eyes could sometimes appear almost insolent. He understood the thoughts that underlay her words, and he appreciated them. But in a sense he was in the same emotional position as she was. He knew her earlier marriage—ended when her husband was killed in the Falklands—had already been a failure before that war, and he was determined that this time she would have as few regrets as possible.

'I'm glad you reminded me, Sergeant,' he said. 'Now, you make us some tea while I do the unpacking. Later we might go for a short walk and see if we can find a pleasant

local. We deserve a couple of drinks before work begins
tomorrow.'

'You mean, you do,' said Hilary. 'Remember—' She
patted her stomach.

'Non-alcoholic drinks are all the rage,' said Tansey.
'They'll do you good.'

They were finishing their tea when the front doorbell rang.
They exchanged surprised glances, but neither of them
moved.

'Who on earth could that be?'

'You don't think it could be your friend—what's her
name? Jean, isn't it?'

Hilary shook her head. It had been a pleasant surprise
to discover that they would be living near Jean Cranworth.
Hilary's family and Jean's had been neighbours when both
the girls were children, and they had gone through school
together. Jean was a couple of years older than Hilary, but
this had never seemed to affect their close friendship. Later,
of course, as they grew up and married, they had inevitably
seen less and less of each other, but they had kept in touch,
and Jean had been delighted to learn that Hilary was coming
to London.

'No, I'm sure it's not her, Dick. It's all arranged. She's
picking me up and I'm having lunch with her tomorrow.
Why should she come round now?'

The bell rang again, firmly and almost demandingly.
Reluctantly, Tansey got to his feet. 'The simplest thing is
to answer the door,' he said, going into the hall.

Curious, Hilary followed him, in time to see the flap of
the letter-box lift and a face peer in. Tansey swung the door
open. The figure of a short squat woman in a purple jumper
and skirt straightened itself, and its owner, apparently in
no way abashed at being caught in such an undignified
posture, looked slowly from Tansey's suede shoes up his

long, lean body to his amused grey eyes. As the purple woman was scarcely five feet tall, this inspection took some time, but she didn't speak until she had subjected Hilary to a similar scrutiny.

Then she said, somewhat formally, 'I am Mrs Meade. You must be Mr and Mrs Tansey. Or do you prefer your rank, sir? Mr Porter preferred to be anonymous, as it were.'

'Mister will be fine,' said Tansey, who had by now placed the little woman. 'You're the caretaker—the porteress—for these flats, aren't you, Mrs Meade? My colleague spoke of you.'

'That's right, and normally I'm not on duty at weekends, except for emergencies, like, but seeing as how you've just arrived I thought I'd better come up to make sure you were settling in all right.'

'How kind of you,' said Hilary.

'You'll need to know the dos and don'ts of the block, too,' said Mrs Meade.

'The house rules,' Tansey murmured. He gestured to the chairs around the hall table. 'Won't you sit down, Mrs Meade?'

'Thank you.' Mrs Meade took plenty of time to make herself comfortable before she continued. 'This is a small block of flats, but it's very conveniently located. You'll soon get to know your way around. We're only a few steps from the shops of the Marylebone High Street, close to Baker Street station, and just a short walk from Oxford Street.'

'So I gather,' said Tansey. 'I'm sure we'll be happy here.'

'Good,' replied Mrs Meade, briskly. 'Now, this block has always been very pleasant and respectable—not like some others I could name—and we try to keep it like that. No noisy parties. No television or radios to be played loudly after midnight. If you happen to come in late you're quiet on the stairs and outside your front door. Same applies if you're seeing guests off.'

'In short, be considerate,' said Tansey, who was becoming somewhat impatient.

Mrs Meade gave him a sharp glance. 'The post and newspapers are delivered to my basement flat, and I bring them round as soon as they arrive,' she went on. 'Or, if you're going to be out, anything can be left with me for pick-up or delivery to you later—like laundry, say. And you let me know at once if a tap's dripping or a light bulb's failed on the stairs or there's any other complaint. And don't hesitate to ask if you've got questions. I deal with problems at once—except, as I said, at weekends, when I should be disturbed only for real emergencies.'

'That all sounds wonderful, Mrs Meade,' said Tansey, pushing back his chair and standing up. 'We'll do our best not to bother you—especially at weekends.'

'Yes, indeed. Thank you very much, Mrs Meade,' Hilary added, giving the little woman a smile. 'It was good of you to come up today.'

Mrs Meade nodded in acknowledgement of the tribute, but she didn't take the hint. It was several moments before she got to her feet and moved slowly towards the door. As she went, she turned and remarked, 'This is one of my favourite floors. Your neighbours are particularly nice people. There's Miss Natalie Smythe in the rear flat. She's an actress, though she's resting at the moment. But you'll probably recognize her. She's been on the telly a lot. And across the way is Mrs Grace Horner, a widowed lady, so friendly, always ready to have a chat; she lives with her son, David, who works in a travel agency. But you'll be meeting them all before long, I'm sure.'

'Dear God!' said Dick Tansey, leaning against the door as it at last closed behind Mrs Meade. 'Do we laugh or cry?'

'Laugh!' Hilary was firm.

'The old harridan! She didn't give a damn whether we

were settling in or not. All she wanted to do was inspect us.'

'Well, it was quite reasonable—and she didn't learn much.'

'She'll be back—and she will—I mean she'll make it her business to learn everything she can about us, darling. I bet she's an authority on the public and private lives of every single inhabitant of these flats.'

'Probably.' Hilary laughed. 'We'll have to be on our best behaviour for the sake of the Porters. But let's get unpacked now, Dick, and then we can go in search of those drinks you promised me—with or without alcohol.'

Several hours later Dick and Hilary Tansey lay in their respective twin beds. They had passed a pleasant evening and Hilary, who had taken a mild sedative, was asleep. Lying on her back, lips parted, she snored softly. The sounds made her husband smile.

He didn't resent the fact that he couldn't sleep; his mind was too active, occupied with thoughts of the next day, which would be his first full day on duty with the Met. He hadn't wanted the assignment but, since the choice had been forced upon him, he was looking forward to it.

The inside of a week spent in London earlier in the month had done much to allay his doubts and fears. He had been given a comprehensive briefing on the workings of the various departments of New Scotland Yard. He was of course aware that the Metropolitan Police District was divided into Areas, which were sub-divided into Divisions. The Area Headquarters at Cannon Row Police Station, close to the site of the old Scotland Yard, dealt with the whole of central London, and Delta Mike Division, based at the Marylebone Police Station in Seymour Street, was where Tansey was to take Detective Chief Inspector Porter's place for a while at what the Yard termed the 'grass roots', in charge of the Divisional CID. Tansey had spent a day with Porter, but it was clear that until he became more closely acquainted with his manor—and with whatever cases were current—he would be heavily dependent on his staff of local CID officers.

The Divisions and the Areas, Tansey knew, could call on the specialist resources of the Yard and—in the case of major crimes—on the Yard's Major Investigations Reserve. Unfortunately, according to Porter, there were usually more major crimes than officers available in the Reserve, so that preliminary inquiries often fell to the CID Chief Inspector in whose Division the crime had occurred. When a murder was concerned this was especially true when a case appeared at first sight to be a so-called 'domestic'.

Tansey had been worked hard during this period of briefing; there had been just time to eat and sleep, and he had returned to Oxfordshire exhausted but exhilarated. Everyone in London had been most helpful. No one had tried to patronize him, and he had not been made to feel an incompetent country cousin, which was an approach he had feared. Indeed, the only disappointment had been that the Porters' child was sick, so that he had been unable to look over the flat that he and Hilary were to occupy. And, seen for the first time that day, he had found it depressing.

It was noisy, too, especially after the relative quiet of Kidlington. Even at one in the morning there was the distant roar of traffic from the Marylebone Road, a main traffic artery. Closer, there was the more irritating hum of a nearby air-conditioner or exhaust fan, and the sound of cars braking and accelerating round an adjacent corner. Suddenly a party of drunks passed by, singing a bawdy song. Maliciously hoping that the drunks had woken Mrs Meade, Tansey got up and shut the window.

As he got back into bed he reminded himself that the next six months were likely to be far more agreeable and gratifying for him than for his wife, and he made a secret promise to make it up to her as soon as he could. Reflecting on this, he drifted into sleep.

CHAPTER 2

Detective Chief Inspector Tansey found it strange to be walking to work, rather than driving his car, but it was a lovely May day, warm for the time of year, and as he strode along Paddington Street in the direction of the Marylebone Police Station, his spirits rose. He hadn't liked leaving Hilary alone in the flat, though he knew this feeling was absurd; her friend, Jean Cranworth, would be picking her up in a couple of hours, and she should have an enjoyable day. He hoped he would, too.

It took him a full four minutes to cross Baker Street. Crowds of commuters, hurrying on foot from Baker Street Station on the corner of the Marylebone Road a few hundred yards to the north, blocked the wide pavement as they surged past. The traffic was a steady flow, and Tansey missed one green light while he glanced around him, and hoped that the distinguished criminological associations of the street represented a good omen.

Across Baker Street, Tansey made his way west and south, intrigued by the variety of small shops selling everything from what seemed to him hideous works of art to the flimsiest of ladies' underwear. The latter made him grin, and he promised himself a slow stroll through the area with Hilary when he had time.

Soon he reached the corner of Seymour Street, and was going up the ramp to the main entrance of the red-brick police station that had been purpose-built comparatively recently to take the place of the old, small, cramped and

decrepit station on Marylebone Lane. He was expected and
made welcome, and taken at once to see the uniformed
Divisional Chief Superintendent, an officer called Peter
Wilson, whom he had met during his recent briefing in
London, and who greeted him now as a valued friend and
colleague.

After routine preliminaries, Chief Superintendent Wilson
passed Tansey over to John Bradbury, the senior CID
inspector, who showed him to a small but bright office
which had previously been Porter's. Outside the office could
be heard the constant ringing of phones, voices calling
to each other, people moving along the corridor—some
obviously on urgent business. For a moment Tansey felt at
something of a loss, but he shook himself and stared at the
pile of files stacked in the in-tray on the desk. Turning to
Bradbury, he remarked, 'I see you're all ready for me.'

'I'm afraid so, sir,' said Bradbury. 'Like everywhere else,
we're short of officers and struggling hard to keep up with
ourselves. Most of the men are out on the job by this time,
so I thought you could meet them later, and I'd start by
briefing you on the cases we've got running. Then I'll tell
you about the narks we've got lined up—in this town we
depend heavily on informers; a lot of the boys have their
own special little friends—and very close about them they
are, too, sir.'

'Fine,' said Tansey. 'Let's dive in.'

But they were immediately interrupted, first by an attractive young woman PC, who reminded Tansey of Hilary and
who brought them coffee and biscuits, and secondly by the
telephone. Bradbury answered it, and passed the receiver
to Tansey. 'It's the Super, sir,' he said.

'I'm sorry to throw you in at the deep end, Chief Inspec-
tor,' said Wilson's voice at the other end of the line, 'but
I've just had a call from Hector Greyling—the Right
Honourable Hector Greyling. He's an important Minister

of the Crown, as I'm sure you know, and he keeps a flat in our patch, in one of those posh terraces that practically surround Regent's Park. Some of the original houses have become offices, a few are still individually owned, but most have been converted to flats—luxurious ones, too.'

'I know of them, sir,' said Tansey.

'Well, this Greyling wants to see a senior detective at once. He's been at his country house with his wife for the weekend, and he says that while they were away he's certain someone tried to break into their flat.'

'Was anything taken?'

'No, apparently not—but, you know, he *is* a Minister—'

'I know,' said Tansey resignedly. 'We have similar situations, even in the Thames Valley.'

Superintendent Wilson laughed. 'Would you mind going over there and keeping him happy? Get Bradbury to find you a car and a driver—I suggest Detective-Sergeant Sester, if he's available.'

Tansey's first impression of Detective-Sergeant Sester was that he was an errant schoolboy. Sester was slight of build, and must just have squeezed in under the wire when he was tested for the regulation minimum height for Metropolitan Police officers. His face was round and smooth, only a small neat gingery moustache proving that his skin wasn't totally innocent of a razor. In fact Sester was in his middle forties, London born and bred, street-wise and with all the wit of a typical Londoner. On many occasions he had found his youthful appearance a great advantage. It was said behind his back—though he was aware of the comment and even boasted of it in the right company—that it was lucky he'd decided to join the Force; otherwise he could easily have become a redoubtable crook.

But as yet Tansey knew nothing of this, and in the short drive to Regent's Park there was little opportunity for conversation. He was aware that Sester was studying him closely before finally venturing the view that London traffic was 'a fair bugger and getting worse every day'. Tansey agreed amiably, and Sester drove around the Park and along the Terrace where the Greylings lived, to draw up in front of one of the tall cream-coloured buildings. As Tansey mentally noted the number on the block, Sester added, a little surprisingly, 'Beautiful, this place, isn't it, sir? D'you know, I'm told the rates for a flat here are more than what I earn in a year.'

'That doesn't astonish me,' said Tansey. 'They're probably more than I earn, too. I didn't realize there was so much money to be made out of politics.'

'It's more than politics with Mr Greyling, sir.' Sergeant Sester, Tansey was to discover, was a mine of information, usually accurate. 'He's one of those property tycoons. Made his millions before he went into Parliament—but nothing known against him,' he added, looking sideways at Tansey to see how the Chief Inspector would take this gratuitous comment. When Tansey made no reply, Sergeant Sester went on, 'Wife's a real looker, half his age. I suppose she went after the money. The first wife got killed in a ski-ing accident. There's a son, but he lives abroad, so he's no bother to dad.'

Tansey, who had rarely heard a better potted biography, stared at Sester and grinned broadly. 'Thanks a lot, Sergeant,' he said. 'Now I've got a much better idea what to expect.'

As Sergeant Sester swung open the car door, and Tansey got out, a man in a black alpaca jacket and striped trousers emerged from the house. He was obviously a very superior porter. 'You can't park here,' he said authoritatively.

Sester took his time, and then murmured softly but very firmly, as if he were addressing a newly recruited constable, 'Police. Detective Chief Inspector Tansey to see Mr

Greyling, at his request.' His voice changed to a bark.
'Show us the way now, please. And keep an eye on the car.'

Once again Tansey grinned as the porter caved in hurriedly. 'Er—yes, sir,' he said. 'If you'll come this way,
gentlemen.' He escorted them through an elegant entrance
hall to a door on the ground floor.

Hector Greyling opened the door to them himself. He
was a big florid-faced man in his late forties, immaculately
tailored and wearing a Guards' tie. He didn't look in the
best of humours, but he made an effort to appear welcoming
as Tansey introduced himself and his sergeant.

'Come along in! Come along in!' he said in a deep,
booming baritone, and led the way into a drawing-room.
'Chief Inspector Tansey, darling, and Detective-Sergeant
Sester,' he added, slightly muting the boom. 'My wife.' He
gestured.

It was a huge room, long and high and furnished in
impeccable taste. Tansey was waved to the comfort of a
huge sofa, while Sergeant Sester perched himself on an
upright chair beside a small table and thoughtfully opened
his notebook. Questioned later by Hilary, Tansey could
only recall the Chinese rugs on the parquet floor and the
painting over the mantel that was almost certainly a Van
Gogh. He managed to listen to the Minister, take in what
he was saying, and even ask the right questions about
security arrangements, but almost all his attention was
focused on Mrs Greyling.

Tansey had never before met such a beautiful woman.
Pamela Greyling was in her middle twenties. She was tall,
slender and elegant, and she moved with the grace of a
dancer—which indeed she had been before her marriage.
But it was her colouring that was so striking. Her hair,
which she wore loose to her shoulders, was literally the
colour of ripe corn, her eyes were a light green and her skin
slightly bronzed as if by sun and sea. Yet somehow she

escaped mere chocolate-box prettiness. Tansey wondered idly how she had come to marry Greyling—money, as Sester had suggested?

'—so you'll understand why I'm anxious, Chief Inspector. It's not merely that we have a great many valuable pieces in this flat. They're relatively unimportant. It's my wife's safety that's paramount. I wanted her to return to the country, where we have our own staff, but she refuses, and I have to leave for a few days to attend meetings in Paris.' Greyling looked at his watch. 'If I don't go soon, I shall miss my flight.'

'Then do go, Hector!' Mrs Greyling failed to keep the edge from her voice. 'I'm sure the Chief Inspector has better things to do than worry about a few footprints in a flowerbed, and a few scratches on the shutters outside my bedroom window.'

Greyling ignored her. 'It's such a pity that this is a ground-floor flat, but we chose it because of the small private garden. Part of the trouble is that there are two means of access to it: through the main entrance—the way you came, of course—and directly from the Terrace along a pathway between this block of flats and the next. Of course, we've got a wrought-iron gate at the front with an alarm on it, but—'

'Can anyone else use this pathway, sir? People from the building next door, for example?'

'No, no. It's completely private. You'll see. The garden's walled, and the wall joins on to the block next door.'

'Yes,' said Tansey. 'What about tradesmen?'

'It's not a tradesmen's entrance in any sense. Their way in is through the basement and up a service lift.'

'Well, sir, your security arrangements would seem excellent,' Tansey said. 'But we'll have a look round, and inspect the marks you mention. If we've any suggestions I'll let you know, and in the meantime I'll arrange for the police patrol to pay extra attention to this Terrace for the next few days.

I'm afraid that's all I can do at the moment. But Mrs Greyling must call me at Marylebone Police Station if there are any further incidents.'

'That will be splendid.' Mrs Greyling spoke dismissively. 'Thank you very much, Chief Inspector. Now, Hector, you must go. Are you all ready? Marie can show the officers around.'

A middle-aged woman, obviously a housekeeper, had appeared in the doorway and, after more thanks from the Minister, Tansey and Sergeant Sester were taken through a kitchen into the small walled garden, totally cut off from the building next door. As Greyling had said, access to it was only from the ground-floor flat itself, or from a tarmac pathway leading to the Terrace and protected at the front by an iron gate.

It was true that there were a few scuffed footprints under a window that they were told gave on to Mrs Greyling's bedroom, and some indeterminate marks around the catch on the wooden shutters with which all the ground-floor windows on this side of the house were equipped. Little could be learnt from them.

That was a pretty unnecessary visit, the Chief Inspector reflected as they got back into their car. But he wondered why Pamela Greyling, who hadn't struck him as a nervous woman, should have seemed so tense and on edge, and so eager for her husband to be gone. Then he dismissed the thought. The Greylings were nothing to him; he doubted if he would hear any more about the incident, or see either of them again.

When Tansey had left their own vastly more modest apartment that morning, Hilary cleared up the breakfast, tidied the flat—an unnecessary chore—and made a brief shopping list. She considered a short expedition to examine the local stores, but decided instead to await her friend.

Jean Cranworth arrived punctually. She was not unlike Hilary in appearance, but shorter and smaller. Her face wore a slightly worried expression, but she greeted Hilary warmly.

'My dear, this is wonderful. I can't tell you how delighted I was when you said you were coming to London. And living so close! We're only about ten minutes' walk away— but you'll see for yourself. I thought we'd have coffee at Madame Sagne's in the High Street and then go home for a light lunch, if that'll suit you.'

Hilary laughed at her friend's enthusiasm. 'It sounds super. But who or what is Madame Sagne?'

'It's the best place in this part of London for coffee and the most mouth-watering cakes. Everyone around goes there —and it's on our way, so what could be better?'

Exchanging news and gossip, the two women walked down Marylebone High Street. They had not seen each other for some time—Jean had been ill and unable to attend Hilary's wedding to Dick Tansey, and they had a lot to talk about. Madame Sagne's turned out to consist of one large room, with a glass-covered counter in front near the display window, and a number of tables at the rear. They were lucky to find one vacant, but even when they were seated with coffee and the cakes they had chosen before them, Jean returned to personal subjects. She seemed to be full of curiosity and asked innumerable questions about Tansey.

'No regrets then, Hilary?' she said.

'None. Dick suits me perfectly.'

'I'm glad for you. May it continue. From the wedding photographs you sent me he seems very good-looking, like my Harry. Don't women find him attractive?'

'I—I've never really thought about it. I know I do.'

'Well, you've not been married long, and maybe your Dick's the faithful kind. Of course a lot depends on temp-

tation and opportunity, doesn't it? I suppose most men have
to be forgiven the odd peccadillo.'

Hilary was disturbed at the direction their conversation
had taken. She had no intention of discussing any private
aspects of her marital life with Jean or anyone else. And
Dick Tansey was certainly not Harry Cranworth, whom she
could easily imagine as a minor Don Juan. Immediately she
recanted her opinion; she scarcely knew Harry and she had
no right to judge him, even secretly.

Tentatively she said, 'Jean, you're still happy with Harry,
aren't you?'

'Oh yes! I wish he didn't have to travel so much, but
that's part of his job. No, Hilary, I was thinking of Steve.'
Jean laughed. Steve Cranworth was Harry's younger
brother. 'You know, it may sound absurd, but once I hoped
you might marry Steve.'

'Good heavens!' Hilary was startled and amused. 'I'm
certain there was never any chance of that.'

'Anyway, I'm glad you didn't. Steve's a dear, but he
does rather flit from lady to lady.' Jean lowered her voice so
that Hilary could barely hear what she was saying. 'That's
his latest, just come in. Actually, this one's lasted longer
than usual for him. He seems to be badly smitten for
once.'

Suddenly an imperious voice was heard above the general
level of conversation of the coffee-drinkers. 'I'm Gemma
Fielding. I ordered a cake for today. Is it ready?'

'Yes, Miss Fielding. Here we are. Waiting for you.' A
woman who was obviously the manageress had moved a
younger salesgirl aside to attend to Miss Fielding herself.

Hilary turned her head to watch as the cake was passed
across the glass counter and duly paid for. Gemma Fielding's appearance fitted her voice. She was tall and striking.
Her hair, straight and short, was the colour of an orange.
Her skin was white and, except for lipstick that matched

her hair, she was devoid of make-up. But it was her clothes that were disconcerting. On this pleasantly warm spring day she wore high black boots and a long black cloak.

'Quite a character, isn't she?' Jean murmured as Miss Fielding departed with a swirl of her cloak.

'Does she always dress in that spectacular fashion?' Hilary asked.

'Yes, as far as I know—even on duty.' Jean smiled. 'In spite of appearances, she's a librarian in the reference department of the Marylebone Public Library.'

'Then perhaps her clothes make up for the lack of glamour in her job,' Hilary suggested. 'Incidentally, I must join that library. Someone told me it's extremely good.'

For a while the conversation became general as Jean expatiated yet again on the many amenities of Marylebone. 'It's one of the best and most convenient parts of London to live in,' she said. 'The shops are excellent. You can get anything you want on the High Street or around. But it's true that many of them keep changing. Very few of those so-called boutiques we passed will last more than a few years, if that. Nevertheless, there are some good food stores —and there's always Selfridges just a few blocks away.'

'It all sounds wonderful,' said Hilary.

'Mind you,' Jean went on, 'a lot's changed, quite apart from the shops, even in the ten years we've lived here. For instance, I wouldn't dream of going out by myself late at night, say to post a letter or to see friends to a car, as I would certainly have done a while ago.'

'Really? Not even in a well-lit street?' Hilary was surprised.

'No. And I advise you to be careful too, my dear. There are a lot of unpleasant people around these days.'

'I'll take care.'

Hilary spoke automatically. Her interest had been caught by a sudden change of tone in Jean's voice, and a slight stiffening in her posture. Hilary let her gaze follow her friend's. The ping of the doorbell had heralded the entrance of another customer, and it was obvious that it was this new arrival who had caused Jean's concern.

It was also a woman, but this time a small woman with a petite, child-like figure and a disproportionately large head. In no sense was this a deformity, and it would have passed unnoticed except by the most attentive observer if the woman hadn't chosen to draw attention to it by having her thick dark hair back-combed so that it stood out like a halo around her face. Her clothes were casual and casually worn, but with such finesse that Hilary found herself assuming that the garments were expensive. Another character, she thought, but found that Jean, having suddenly murmured that it was time to go, was already collecting her handbag and the bill, and was making for the cashier's desk.

Hilary followed more slowly. The newcomer was standing in the doorway, looking around as if she were expecting to see a friend. Someone at the rear of the room waved to her and, smiling, she moved forward. In the narrow space in front of the counter, she and Jean couldn't avoid meeting. To Hilary's surprise they greeted each other like dear friends.

'Jean! How very nice. We haven't seen you for ages and ages.'

'Hello, Catherine. How are you? As you say, it's been a long time.'

This fairly meaningless conversation continued for a couple of minutes as Catherine asked after Harry and Jean asked after Donald, presumably Catherine's husband. Hilary was introduced briefly as 'my old friend, Mrs Tansey', and learnt that Catherine was a Mrs Brooke-Brown. Catherine volunteered that they must all get together very soon, and Jean agreed. Then, after a flurry of goodbyes Hilary and Jean were walking down the High Street towards

Manchester Square, where the Cranworths had their maisonette.

'Does Mrs Brooke-Brown live around here?' Hilary asked innocently.

'Well, not terribly far away. They have a mews house, very attractive, near Portland Place. Donald's something in the City. I'm not sure what, but I doubt if it matters. Catherine has plenty of money.'

Jean spoke off-handedly, but clearly the subject was distasteful to her for some reason she apparently had no wish to explain. Hilary took her cue and began to talk of other matters.

CHAPTER 3

The Chief Inspector was struggling to put his key into the unfamiliar lock on the front door of his flat when he heard a door open behind him, and a contralto voice say, 'You must be Mr Tansey.'

At least, he thought, whoever it was had not had the impudence to announce his profession or his rank. He turned, and was confronted by an elderly lady in the doorway opposite. His mind still on the events of the day, he was for a moment slightly nonplussed. Then he realized that she must be the neighbour of whom Mrs Meade had spoken.

He said, 'Yes. I'm Dick Tansey.'

'And I'm Grace Horner.'

Mrs Horner, Tansey guessed, was in her early seventies, but might have been ten years younger. She had a neat and upright figure, and she obviously spent a good deal of time cherishing her appearance. There was the faintest pink tint in her well-groomed hair—a tint that was reflected in the rims of her fashionably large spectacles and matched her pink lipstick and nail varnish.

'I called—except that I suppose that's too high-falutin' a word for merely ringing the opposite bell—I tried to call on your wife this morning, but she was out. I just wanted to bid you welcome, and say that if there's anything David —he's my son—or I can do to make your stay here more enjoyable, we'd be only too happy to help. Don't hesitate to ask.'

'That's—that's extremely kind of you, Mrs Horner.'

'Not a bit. It's a common fallacy that there's no neigh-bourliness in London. That simply isn't true, you know. I'm sure you've heard the comment that London's a collection of little villages, and within each there's a great deal of camaraderie.'

'Yes, indeed.'

Tansey was wondering how to make a polite escape from this rather overpowering female when he heard steps run up the stairs. Almost immediately a man in a dark grey suit appeared. Mrs Horner's introduction was unnecessary. Although the new arrival was almost a foot taller than his mother, his features—the bright brown eyes and the thin nose—left no room for doubt that this was David. He offered Tansey a slightly damp hand.

'Hello, sir. I'm sure my mother's said it, but I hope you and Mrs Tansey are settling in OK.'

'Yes. Indeed. But if you'll excuse me—' Tansey seized his chance. 'It's been a long day—'

'Of course, Mr Tansey. Of course. Come along, David,' said Mrs Horner, as if her son had been responsible for detaining Tansey. 'Tell your wife I'll be in touch,' she added as Tansey at last got his key in the lock.

'Yes, of course, Mrs Horner. Very many thanks. Goodbye for now,' he said over his shoulder.

But it was not until they were having supper that Tansey

remembered to deliver Mrs Horner's message to Hilary. They seemed to have an extraordinary amount of information to exchange with each other—starting with Tansey's first day at his new post, which in view of Hilary's professional interest he described in detail.

'If I couldn't have you with me, darling, Sergeant Sester is the next best thing,' he said. 'He's a character, and a knowledgeable one. I guess he'll be a fine acquisition.'

Hilary laughed, and Tansey went on to tell her of the Right Honourable Hector Greyling and his luscious wife. 'To be honest,' he concluded,' I don't think their establishment would suit us. It's just *too* luxurious.'

'But the Cranworths' would,' said Hilary at once. 'As soon as Harry gets back from his current business trip, Jean wants us to go to dinner with them, so you'll see it. It's a converted house with offices on the two lower floors. Jean and Harry have a maisonette on the next two floors, and Steve—that's Harry's brother, lives in a flat under the eaves. They were terribly lucky to be able to buy a long lease on the maisonette and the flat. It's ideal for them.'

'Doesn't that sort of place mean a lot of stairs?' Dick Tansey had not met any of the Cranworths and wasn't really interested in them or their establishment.

'No. They've a private lift. The whole place is awfully well arranged. And from the front rooms there's a wonderful outlook over the garden of Manchester Square, with the Wallace Collection building in the background.'

'And the blessing of no neighbours after office hours, I suppose,' said Tansey. 'Which reminds me, Hilary.' He recounted his meeting with the Horners, and passed on Mrs Horner's message. 'I shouldn't encourage her too much,' he added. 'She looks the type who might take to popping in, and you know what you feel about that sort of thing.'

'I certainly won't. Incidentally, when I got back from Jean's this afternoon, I met our other neighbour, Natalie

Smythe, the actress. I recognized her at once, though she looks a bit different on the telly.'

'Is she pleasant?'

'A charmer. She asked us to have a drink with her over the weekend, but I said it would depend on your work. And she's promised to take me to a TV studio to watch her making some commercials. It should be fun.'

'Whew!' Dick Tansey laughed. 'We've only been in London about twenty-four hours and invitations are pouring in. Whoever said this was a lonely place?'

At that moment there were many who would claim with some justice that London was lonely, or would have admitted that they were personally lonesome. After their lengthy conversation during the day, with its unexpressed undertones, Hilary would not have been altogether surprised to learn that among these individuals was Jean Cranworth. Jean hadn't heard from her husband in two days and had no idea when he was likely to return. She didn't dare to telephone his firm; once before she had done that and Harry had been furious. She tried Steve, but got no answer, though she could hear his phone ringing in the empty flat above.

Somehow spending the day with Hilary and hearing the happiness in her voice when she spoke of Dick and the baby they were expecting had induced in Jean a mood of frustration stronger than her usual mild discontent. On an impulse she went into the room that Harry called his study. He wasn't a tidy man, and it took her a minute to find what she was seeking—the phone number of the hotel in Paris where he was staying.

At least, she thought with some bitterness, she knew that this time he had gone to Paris alone, because she had herself driven him to the airport, and he had made no secret of the name of his hotel. She tapped out the phone number, and waited.

Monsieur Cranworth was no longer in the hotel, she was told. No, there could be no question of a mistake. He had indeed been a guest, but he had left that morning to catch the noon flight from Charles de Gaulle airport for London.

With a sigh she replaced the receiver, wishing she had never made that call. It was better not to know. If Harry had caught the noon flight, he should have been home long ago, even if he had gone straight from the airport to his office—and in that event he would surely have called her to announce his safe return. Of course he might have come back to London and gone—Where? To whom? She knew that she was torturing herself, but she couldn't help it.

Jean helped herself to a glass of sherry, and then another. She made herself a scratch meal from the remains of the luncheon she had given Hilary, and watched television. Time passed slowly. She tried Steve again, but again there was no answer. Her phone rang once, but it was merely someone trying to get in touch with Harry or Steve.

At ten-fifteen she telephoned the Brooke-Browns. A voice she recognized as Donald's answered and she asked for Catherine. But Catherine, he said, was not at home.

'Who is that?' the voice inquired. 'Can I take a message?'

Jean put down the instrument without answering. She thought that he had probably guessed her identity, but she didn't care. She had a bath and got ready for bed.

At eleven o'clock the doorbell rang.

Jean ran to the entry-phone. For one wild moment she thought it might be Harry, having mislaid his keys, or more likely Steve. But it was neither of them.

'Mrs H. Cranworth?' someone asked.

'Yes. I'm Mrs Cranworth. Who's that?' Jean demanded. The entry-phone always distorted voices. 'Who's that?' she repeated, suddenly afraid that Harry might have met with

an accident and this was a policeman or some bearer of bad
tidings.

'I have a delivery for you, Mrs Cranworth. I'm sorry to
be so late, but it was taken to the wrong address and the
lady brought it back to us.'

'What is it? Are you sure it's for me? I'm not expecting
anything—'

'Yes, ma'am. It's for you, if you're Mrs H. Cranworth.
It's flowers.'

'Flowers! Oh, well.' Jean's relief made her forget all
the warnings she had expressed to Hilary over coffee that
morning. 'All right. Bring them up.' She pushed the button
to release the outer door. 'You'll see the lift right in front of
you. It's the first stop.'

She put down the entry-phone, made sure that the belt
of her gown was tied tightly, and went to the front door of
the maisonette. When she heard the clang of the lift gate
she opened it. Outside stood the delivery man, in motorcycle
gear, and wearing a helmet so that she couldn't see his face.
But her eyes had gone instinctively to the long white box
that the man was carrying. There was green writing on it,
and an illustration of a spray of flowers.

'Thank you very much,' she said.

She was totally unprepared for what happened next. As
she took the box into her hands the man moved towards
her, crowding her back into the hall. She had no time to
protest. As her head came up she found herself staring at a
pistol.

'Turn around,' he said, 'and walk slowly up to the bedroom.'

Jean turned, but for a moment she was incapable of
movement. She stood, her heart thudding and her mind
racing uselessly. She couldn't believe what was happening.
But the sound of the front door being shut behind her broke
her trance. The finality of the noise made her position all

too clear and, illogically because she knew that there was no one in the building and no possibility that she might be heard, she opened her mouth to scream. Immediately she felt a hard glove close over her mouth and the barrel of the pistol between her shoulder-blades.

'Shut up and walk!'

Jean obeyed, though she was shaking. Suddenly she no longer cared. This man, this stranger with his box of flowers —flowers? The irony of it—was going to rape her and then kill her. There was no doubt. She was going to die and there was nothing—absolutely nothing—that she could do about it. But why? He must be mad. She had never hurt him, or anyone else for that matter. Why should he want to destroy her?

She had reached the foot of the stairs that led to the upper floor of the maisonette when she remembered that the man had said '*up*' to the bedroom. Was this chance, merely a way of expressing himself? Or had the man known that this was a maisonette and not a flat on one floor?

Then an explanation hit her, an unpalatable revelation that she did her best to avoid. There were no names beside the bells by the front door—only numbers: '1' for the maisonette, and '2' for Steve's flat. But the man had known her name. He had said specifically that the flowers were for Mrs H. Cranworth. Clearly he was no madman. He had come—been sent—to kill Jean Cranworth, Harry's wife.

Without realizing what she was doing Jean had climbed the stairs and reached the threshold of the bedroom. Tears were streaming down her cheeks. She was unaware that the pressure of the gun between her shoulder-blades had eased, and she was taken by surprise when a wire was slipped over her head and drawn viciously tight. There was just one moment of agony, and then she knew no more.

*

Less than ten minutes later the killer quietly let himself out of the maisonette. He was now carrying a black plastic bag into which he had put the box of flowers. He had no reason to expect any trouble, but he kept the jacket of his motorcycle gear open, and his pistol readily accessible in the pocket of his slacks.

He went down in the lift to the ground floor, then opened the front door a slit and peered outside. This, he knew, was a dangerous moment. He must not be seen leaving the building. In his helmet, he couldn't be identified, but he could be described, and now that the crime was committed he felt nervous and vulnerable. He was fairly confident that no one had seen him talking on the entry-phone and going into the house. He had done his best to satisfy himself that the woman would be alone by means of a phone call asking for either Harry or Steve Cranworth; his victim had been totally forthcoming—her husband was away overnight and she believed his brother was out for the evening.

And once inside the building the operation had gone smoothly. If anything had seemed wrong—an unexpected visitor, maybe—he would merely have delivered the flowers —bought in South London in a busy florist's where he would be unidentifiable—and left; Jean would merely have thought that the delivery of a box of drooping blooms was someone's idea of a bad joke.

The Square was quiet. He waited while a couple of cars went by, then slipped out of the house. His motorbike was parked across the road, by the railings of the Square's central garden. He put the plastic bag and the pistol into the bike's pannier, and was about to mount the machine when a couple of drunks, singing lustily, seemed to appear from nowhere. He cowered in the shadows until they had passed, and two minutes later he was on his way.

CHAPTER 4

It was Steve Cranworth who called the police.

He dialled 999, waited for what seemed an inordinate length of time, received the query, 'Fire, Police, Ambulance?' and suffered the usual struggle with the operator who, in accordance with the regulations, insisted on securing his phone number before putting him through.

The Information Room at New Scotland Yard answered almost immediately. Steve Cranworth gave his name and address and said, slowly and distinctly, without undue emphasis or emotion, 'My sister-in-law, Mrs Jean Cranworth, has been murdered. Will someone please come?'

The officer who received this message registered that Mr Steve Cranworth had sounded a pretty cool customer, and he reported this information. At the time he said, intentionally impassively, 'Thank you, sir. You are at the address you gave, with the body?'

'Yes, I'm here, and my brother Harry, Mrs Cranworth's husband, is here too. And there's no doubt that Mrs Cranworth is dead.'

'I see, sir. Thank you. Just stay where you are. There's a car on the way.'

At first sight, the death of Jean Cranworth appeared to be a domestic issue, and the case was immediately referred to Delta Mike Division, so that normally Detective Chief Inspector Porter would have found himself in charge. Thus it was that Dick Tansey was faced with the unenviable task of looking into the death of Hilary's friend.

He protested briefly, but in vain, to his Area Detective Chief Superintendent, pointing out the unfortunate coincidence that his wife had been lunching with Jean Cranworth only the previous day. The Chief Superintendent, his man-power limitations in mind, satisfied himself that Mrs Tansey had no relationship with the deceased beyond friendship and that Tansey himself had not met the deceased or her family. Finally, he reached the conclusion that Tansey's remote acquaintance with some of the main characters in the case might prove to be an advantage rather than represent any conflict of interest. So, accompanied by Sergeant Sester, Tansey set off for Manchester Square.

By the time they reached it, the house was already brist-ling with activity. A scene of crime inspector had been despatched from the Yard with his team. The police doctor had officially pronounced Jean dead, and routine photo-graphs had been taken. The pathologist, who had arrived on the scene with unaccustomed speed, was now with the body. Door-handles, the exterior and interior of the lift and any other likely surfaces were being dusted for fingerprints; Harry and Steve Cranworth had offered no objection to providing sample prints for comparison, and they were both waiting in the sitting-room to be interviewed.

The inspector gave an outline of the set-up in the house, of which Tansey had to pretend to be unaware. 'The two lower floors are offices,' the officer said. 'Mr Harry Cran-worth and the deceased live in the two-floored maisonette above, and Mr Steve Cranworth—that's Harry's brother, the man who called the Yard—has a flat at the top of the building.'

Tansey nodded and the inspector took him and his sergeant up to Jean and Harry Cranworth's bedroom. The pathologist had completed his preliminary examination and was washing his hands. He greeted Sergeant Sester like an old friend, and the inspector introduced Tansey.

'Ah, you must be Bill Porter's substitute?' the pathologist said at once.

'That's right,' Tansey agreed.

'And just like him, you'll want all the answers before a poor man's had time to turn around, I suppose?'

'Right again,' Tansey said. He had taken an immediate liking to this red-haired young Scotsman with his obviously assumed air of indifference. He turned to the bed, where the body lay under a sheet. 'What can you tell me?'

The pathologist drew back the sheet. 'This was how she was when I first saw her. In nightgown and robe and lying on her back on top of the duvet. See the mark round her neck?'

How could anyone help seeing the red weal? thought Tansey. In life, Jean Cranworth had been an attractive woman; in death, her face purple and her eyes staring, she was a sight to be avoided.

The pathologist was continuing. 'It's fairly obvious how the wee lassie died. Some unkind person—it could be a woman, for it wouldn't need a lot of strength—garrotted her. Come to think of it, it's an interesting way of killing. Useful, too. Quick. Silent. Easy to make—a garrotte, I mean—just some wire and two bits of wood—and you can simply leave it behind. Here it is. Your people have had a go at it, and I'm taking charge of it till after the PM, if that's all right. But I can't believe it's going to help the inquiry much.'

'As far as we can tell from the carpet, she was killed in the doorway,' the inspector said as Tansey examined the homemade weapon in its plastic envelope. He pointed to a number of chalk circles surrounding scuff marks on the carpet. 'She was probably caught before she fell to the ground, and carried to the bed.'

'Not dragged?' Tansey queried.

'No, sir. At least, there are no further marks to suggest it, though both the Cranworth men have been in here since.

I wouldn't swear to it, but I guess she was carried from the doorway.'

Tansey nodded, and turned back to the pathologist, who had covered the body again and was preparing to depart. 'Just two questions for now,' he said. 'One, the approximate time—I won't quote it against you—and two, any signs of rape or sexual interference?'

'To answer your second question first, absolutely none of the usual signs of sexual attack.' The pathologist shrugged. 'In the first place, as you can see, she was in her night clothes when she was killed, but there was no sign they'd been disarranged in any way. I suppose the assailant might have been interrupted—telephone, doorbell, who knows?'

'Quite,' said Tansey, who didn't need to be reminded of the obvious.

'As to time,' the pathologist continued. 'I don't mind giving you a guess. Between ten last night and three this morning. Not much help, I know, but I'll try to do better later, after the PM.' He produced a wide and savage grin, showing oddly discoloured teeth. 'And I'll throw in something else for free. The lassie might not have gone willingly, but she didn't put up any struggle. Her fingernails might have been manicured this morning.'

'I see,' said Tansey. Then he thanked the pathologist and let the inspector see him out. There was nothing he and Sester could do in the bedroom except get in the way of the experts, who were struggling, like eager hounds, to collect blood, hairs—anything that might conceivably be of forensic interest.

'We'll go and talk to the Cranworth brothers,' Tansey said to Sester.

The sergeant grinned. 'You make them sound like a double act, sir,' he said.

'Let's hope they're not.' Tansey was grim. 'I don't feel

like comics after the sight of that poor woman, and I'm not looking forward to telling my wife about it.'

Harry and Steve Cranworth might have been twins. They were both tall, dark and extremely good-looking. Their looks, together with their casual air of superiority, had on more than one occasion caused them to be mistaken for celebrities—film-stars or television personalities, perhaps. This amused them, but they were both fully prepared to take advantage of the blessings they had been born with. Nevertheless, though Harry was not the most faithful of husbands and Steve enjoyed a succession of affaires, they were both hard-working citizens. Harry, the older by two years, worked for a firm of exporters, and Steve was in publishing.

Neither of them made a favourable first impression on the two detectives, when the uniformed constable who had been waiting with them let the officers into the room. Harry was lying on a sofa, his face and head covered by a cushion, his body moving gently in a regular rhythm. That he could sleep at such a time—when his wife lay upstairs brutally murdered—disgusted Tansey, who was not aware that Harry Cranworth had scarcely slept for the last twenty-four hours and was suffering from exhaustion as well as shock.

At first Tansey found Steve Cranworth even more annoying. He was awake, but was staring out of the window with the headset of a pocket radio or cassette-player clamped over his ears, seemingly lost in a world of his own, and unaware that anyone had entered the room. Sergeant Sester went across and tapped him none too gently on the shoulder.

'Police!' said the sergeant.

'Sorry!' Steve Cranworth, obviously startled, removed his headset and turned down the volume control on the black box he held in his hand. 'Harry!' he shouted at his brother. 'Wake up, Harry! Here are the police again.'

'Sorry,' Steve Cranworth repeated. 'I didn't hear you. In moments of stress I find that music is a good sedative—'

'Classical or pop?' asked Sergeant Sester suddenly.

Steve Cranworth stared at him. 'Why, classical, of course —the three "Bs" usually. But what's—'

'Never mind,' said Tansey. As the older Cranworth groaned and sat up, Tansey nodded his dismissal to the constable standing by the door. He introduced himself and his sergeant, offered condolences on Jean Cranworth's death, and remarked that unfortunately he would have to ask a lot of questions. Neither of the brothers responded. Nor, Tansey was pleased to notice, had they shown any reaction to his name; he had no wish to get involved in a discussion of Hilary's friendship with Jean, irrelevant though it was. He glanced at Sergeant Sester, who was seated on a chair in a quiet corner of the room studying his notebook, and began.

'First, tell me who found Mrs Cranworth, and when and how,' he said.

'We both did,' said Harry.

'Not exactly.' Steve corrected him. 'Harry went into the bedroom—to say good morning and that he was off to his office—so he found her. But he called to me at once, and I ran upstairs, perhaps a minute later.'

Tansey was confused. 'Let me get this straight,' he said. He turned to Harry. 'You didn't sleep in this maisonette last night, I gather. Why not?'

Harry eyed the Chief Inspector a little dubiously, as if he suspected some hidden implication behind this question. Then he said, 'Oh, it's not that unusual. When I get back from a trip very late and don't want to disturb Jean, I often spend the night upstairs in my brother's flat—I've got a key to it, just as Steve's got a key to our maisonette. Anyway, that's what happened last night. I had to go to Paris for my firm and I flew back yesterday. The wretched flight was late, and I had difficulty getting a taxi, so I did what I've often done before.'

'Your wife wasn't expecting you?' Tansey interrupted.

'No. I wasn't sure when I could get home. It all depended on my Paris contacts and I—I didn't want to disappoint her.'

Somehow this last answer didn't ring true to Tansey, but he made no comment. He had as yet no reason to doubt the Cranworths, and only his instinct told him they were not being totally frank—were not telling him the truth, the whole truth and nothing but the truth. After all, they had had plenty of time before the arrival of the police to concoct any story they might like.

He turned to Harry again. 'I understand, Mr Cranworth,' he said. 'Now, perhaps you'd tell me when you last saw your wife alive, and then describe the events of this morning. I'll stop you if I've any questions.'

Harry eyed the Chief Inspector even more dubiously, but when Steve looked as if he were about to make some protest, gestured to prevent him. 'No, no. I'm all right. Naturally, this has been a shock, a hell of a shock, but—'

Harry paused and swallowed. 'I last saw Jean, alive that is, on Wednesday, before I went to Paris. That's almost six days ago. She—she drove me to the airport.'

'So this morning?' Tansey prompted.

'As I said, I spent last night upstairs in my brother's flat. This morning we had breakfast together and then came downstairs. I went to see Jean, and found—found—'

As Harry buried his face in his hands, Tansey turned his attention to Steve. 'You were in your flat last night—when your brother arrived, and until this morning.'

'Yes,' replied Steve shortly. 'I spent the evening reading and listening to music.'

By this time Harry seemed to have recovered his composure, so that Tansey was able to address both the Cran-

worths. 'Did you—either of you—hear any unusual noise
in the building? For instance, the downstairs doorbell or the
lift?' He turned to Steve. 'Did you hear the lift at all—when
your brother arrived, for instance? Think, Mr Cranworth.'

Slowly Steve shook his head. 'These are old houses, which
means they're well-built and, apart from the clang of the
gate, the lift is pretty silent. No, I don't remember hearing
anything.'

'You have keys to this maisonette?'

'Yes, of course, just as Harry and Jean have always
had keys to this place—' Steve stopped abruptly. 'Chief
Inspector, what are you getting at? If you're suggesting that
I went downstairs, killed Jean and then went to bed, you
must be out of your mind. In hell's name, why should I?'

Tansey ignored this outburst. 'There's no sign of a forced
entry,' he said mildly. 'Either Mrs Cranworth let her killer
in voluntarily, or he had a key. Who else might have a key?'

Harry answered. 'Anyone working in the offices on the
lower floors could have keys to the building, and there's a
cleaning woman who looks after the stairs and the hall. But
only the three of us should have keys to the maisonette.'

'And you've got your keys? How many?

'Two for each door—an ordinary Yale and a mortice
lock.'

Both men fished in their pockets and produced key-
tainers. They each showed their keys to the Chief Inspector,
which as far as Tansey could tell matched the keys that had
been found in Jean's handbag on her bedside table. Tansey
changed the subject abruptly.

'Did you telephone your wife while you were in Paris, Mr
Cranworth?'

'Er—yes. Once. On Friday, to say I wouldn't be home
till the following week. I wasn't sure when I'd be able to
make it.'

'Were you close—as a couple, I mean?'

'For heaven's sake, Chief Inspector! Jean and I have been married ten years. Like any other couple, we had the occasional row, but we got—got—on well enough together. We've no children to worry about, so if we hadn't we could easily have got divorced. I wouldn't have needed to kill her.'

'I'm quite aware of that, Mr Cranworth.' Tansey stood up. 'No one's accusing you of anything—either of you. But these questions are necessary.'

'You surprise me,' Harry muttered, just loudly enough for Tansey to hear.

'I'm afraid we'll have to ask you to sign formal statements later,' the Chief Inspector continued, 'but I won't worry you any more for now, except that I'd like to look around this floor, and the flat upstairs.'

The brothers exchanged exasperated glances, but raised no objection. Tansey made a cursory inspection of the maisonette's dining-room, small study and kitchen. He noted that there was a rubbish shaft, but no back door. After a word with Tansey, Sergeant Sester disappeared.

'You say that nothing's missing?' Tansey said to Harry, who had been following him around.

'Nothing obvious. The silver's there, and so's the TV and the video and the hi-fi equipment. I don't know about Jean's jewellery. It didn't occur to me to look. But she doesn't have a great deal, and we never keep much cash in the place. Anyway, Chief Inspector, why choose us to burgle? I should think there are heaps of other flats and houses much less difficult to break into.'

Tansey nodded sombrely. He had thought of that point. He had also thought that if either of the brothers had decided to kill Jean Cranworth they had chosen an odd plan and an even odder method. And yet . . .

Steve showed him up to the flat above the maisonette. It consisted of one large main room that stretched the depth of the house with windows front and back, a small bedroom, a bathroom and a kitchenette. These were all untidy, with piles of books scattered around and an elaborate music centre that took up considerable space on one wall. To Tansey it seemed an obvious bachelor's domain, comfortable and desirable, and almost certainly expensive. He remembered Hilary's comment that the Cranworths had been able to buy a long lease on this maisonette and flat. Certainly they didn't seem to lack money. Tansey made a mental note to inquire into its source.

In the bedroom the bed had been pulled together, but not properly made. In the living-room a duvet and a pillow on the sofa showed where Harry had presumably slept. There were also signs that, as they had said, the Cranworth brothers had breakfasted together; cups, saucers, plates— two of each—had been swilled and stacked on the draining-board beside the sink in the kitchenette. Tansey could see nothing that failed to corroborate the Cranworths' story.

Returning to the living-room, Tansey went to look out of a front window. He stared thoughtfully across the central gardens at the red brick and white stone façade of the Wallace Collection, with its porticoed entrance and tall iron railings protecting the small forecourt. By now there was a steady flow of traffic around the Square and a certain number of pedestrians, but the police presence didn't seem to be causing much interest. At night, he thought, the place would be quiet, so that the chance of witnesses was not good. He was turning away when he noticed a man with a small dog come out of the gardens, and lock the gate behind him.

'Does everyone who lives in the Square have access to the garden?' he asked.

Steve Cranworth was surprised by the question. 'I've no idea. Harry has a key and I suppose we could use it, but who would want to? There are cars parked all the way round the place, and it must stink of petrol fumes.'

As he stopped speaking a doorbell sounded, and Steve involuntarily lifted his head, though he made no comment. Tansey, who had instructed Sergeant Sester to ring the bell that Jean Cranworth might have answered, also ignored the sound. But he was satisfied. The bell could be heard clearly in the flat above—unless of course Steve had his headset on.

He thanked Steve for showing him around his flat, and apologized again for having to intrude at such a time. Then after a few words with the inspector in charge of the scene of crime team he went to find Sester, who was waiting by the car. He badly wanted to speak to Hilary, and wished now that he had paid more attention to her chatter about Jean the previous day.

But he decided that would have to wait. 'Back to the Station, Sergeant,' he said. 'We'll have to get on to Area, but I expect they'll tell us to establish an Incident Room at Seymour Street.'

CHAPTER 5

The routine went into action smoothly. As Tansey had expected, he was authorized to continue with the case for the time being, and to establish his Incident Room in Seymour Street. He briefed officers, who set out on door-to-door interviews with residents of Manchester Square and workers in the offices in the area. An appeal was put out for anyone who had been passing through the Square during the quiet hours of the night of Monday to Tuesday and had seen anything even vaguely suspicious to come forward, though this approach was acknowledged to be unlikely to bear fruit immediately.

Nevertheless, by the end of the day Tansey had learnt a

great deal more about Jean Cranworth, her husband and her brother-in-law, and had collated a lot of information that might or might not prove relevant to the investigation. He had also had a stroke of luck—in the form of a Mr Julian Arbuthnot.

Mr Arbuthnot was the man whom he had seen from the window of Steve Cranworth's flat walking his dog in the central garden of the Square early that morning. There had been no difficulty in tracing him; both he and his small brown poodle lived in the Square and were well-known characters in the district. The luck arose from the fact that Mr Arbuthnot, though in his eighties, was both intelligent and also intensely curious about his neighbours.

'I'm not ashamed of my curiosity,' he said to Tansey, who was interviewing him in the living-room of his first-floor flat. Arbuthnot crossed one brown-clad leg over the other and settled himself comfortably in what was obviously his favourite chair. He was clearly anticipating a lengthy and fascinating conversation. 'Since my dear wife's death, Wellington—that's my poodle—and I have lived alone, and we find very little to entertain us—except other people's foibles. So please don't apologize for causing me any trouble, Chief Inspector, because you're not. I was delighted when your sergeant here said you would want to speak to me yourself. It's all most exciting—Murder in Manchester Square!'

He gave Sester a broad beam, which was not returned. Wellington had taken a sudden and intense interest in the sergeant's leg, and Sester was obviously fearful that the poodle was about to mistake it for a tree.

Tansey took advantage of this break in Arbuthnot's flow of words, and said, 'Sir, you often walk your dog in the Square and its central garden. Yesterday evening—'

'Yes. To think I might have seen the man who killed that nice lady. She was so kind, you know, was Mrs Cranworth. She always stopped to have a word with me when we

met, and sometimes she produced a bone for Wellington.
Wellington loves bones.'

'Mr Arbuthnot!'

'I'm sorry. I'm afraid I'm waffling, Chief Inspector. It's
my turn to apologize.'

'Never mind, sir. You mentioned that you might have
seen a certain man. Tell me about the incident.'

'Last night I was just coming out of the garden with
Wellington when we saw a man in a motorcycle outfit
standing outside the house where the Cranworths live. He
was big, as big as you, Chief Inspector, but I couldn't give
you any better description because he had on one of those
helmets. Wonderful disguises, aren't they, especially at any
distance?' Mr Arbuthnot's thoughts suddenly seemed to
stray.

'What was he doing?'

'The man? Oh, just standing. Then the door opened—
someone inside must have released it—and he went in.'

'Did you see him come out?'

'No. Wellington had done his duty, so I locked the garden
gate and we came home.'

'Now, let's tackle the timing, Mr Arbuthnot? Can you be
precise about it?'

'Perhaps I can, Chief Inspector. My clock here was
striking eleven as Wellington and I came in, but it's usually
five or ten minutes slow. I'd say the man went into the
house at almost exactly eleven o'clock.'

'What makes you certain it wasn't either of the Mr
Cranworths, sir? One of them might have forgotten his key,
and they'd both fit your description.'

'They would indeed, but—'

He was interrupted by a sharp yelp from Wellington.
Sergeant Sester had got tired of the poodle's obsessive
interest, and had aimed a neatly-concealed kick at him. The
dog skittered across the room to its owner, who glanced

suspiciously at the sergeant. Sester returned the glance, his round baby face totally innocent.

Tansey, who had no doubt about what had happened, coughed. 'Mr Arbuthnot, sir, you were about to tell us why—'

'Of course I couldn't swear it wasn't one of the Cranworths,' the old man said testily, picking up Wellington and settling the small poodle on his lap. 'But why should he have been wearing those clothes? Anyway, it can't have been Harry because he's been off on a trip—to Paris, Mrs Cranworth told me—and I saw him come back this morning. Shortly before seven, that was. I saw him pay off the taxi-driver and let himself in. He had his bag and his briefcase with him, so I guessed he'd just arrived and come straight from the airport.'

'Shortly before seven, you say?' Tansey managed to conceal his excitement.

'Yes. My alarm always goes at six-thirty or thereabouts. I throw on some old clothes, and take Wellington straight out. It's a good habit for both of us.'

'I suppose you didn't see Steve Cranworth yesterday or early this morning?' Tansey asked tentatively.

'No. I haven't seen him since Saturday. We met in the greengrocer's in the High Street, shopping.'

Tansey nodded. He wasn't displeased with this answer. It dispelled a vague feeling of apprehension that Mr Arbuthnot might have been inventing or at least embroidering his story in order to appear interesting. But he had made no effort to include Steve in the tale, as he might have done.

'You've been an enormous help to us, sir,' he said. 'We'll get your statement typed, and Sergeant Sester will bring it round for you to read and sign. That is, unless you'd prefer to stroll over to Seymour Street and see the new Police Station.'

At once Mr Arbuthnot was intrigued. 'I should like that,

Chief Inspector. Just phone me and tell me when you want me.'

'We will, sir. Now, before we go, is there anything else you recall that might be relevant?'

Mr Arbuthnot considered. 'No-o. I don't think so. You don't want mere impressions.'

'We might. What is it?' Tansey did his best to suppress his hopes.

'Well, this person I saw go into the Cranworths' house last night,' Mr Arbuthnot said slowly. 'I got an impression —it might have been because of the gear he was wearing —that he was some kind of delivery man. You know, you see them all over London all the time on their wretched motorcycles with their radio telephones screeching. Anyway, I'm nearly sure he was carrying a box, long and white and not heavy. I remember thinking at the time that it was late to be delivering flowers—but that was only a passing hunch. And, as I said, Chief Inspector, I can't vouch for any of this. It was just an impression . . .'

'That bloody dog!' exclaimed Sergeant Sester when he and Tansey were in the street. 'I'll have to have my slacks cleaned.'

Tansey grinned unsympathetically. 'I dare say you'll find some way of charging it up to expenses. And if it weren't for that bloody dog as you call it, Sergeant, Mr Arbuthnot wouldn't have been walking in the Square when he was, and we'd be minus some useful evidence. No, Wellington deserves our thanks—a bone, perhaps. Bear it in mind.'

Sester muttered something under his breath which Tansey affected not to hear. 'Sergeant, I know it's a long shot, but see what you can do about this possible delivery man. Try flower shops in the neighbourhood to start with, and then extend the search. Try the so-called courier firms that operate motorcycles, too. And see if anyone connected with the case has a licence to operate a motorbike—presumably the man was riding more than a small scooter. Get what help you can. And check if there were any fresh flowers or a box at the Cranworths'.'

'Yes, sir. But I'm not hopeful—'

'Nor am I,' admitted Tansey. 'Finding out exactly when Harry Cranworth actually arrived home should prove a simpler task.'

The Chief Inspector had spoken without thinking, as he realized a while later. True, by then he had discovered that both Harry and Steve Cranworth had lied to him, but he had also discovered that their lies led to no firm conclusions.

In fact, Harry Cranworth had arrived at Heathrow from Paris, not as he had said on a delayed last flight on Monday, but at lunch-time on that day. Not only was his name on the passenger manifesto, but he was a familiar figure in the Executive Lounge at the airport. On his arrival he had gone there to inquire about a gold pen he thought he had left behind when he flew out. He was right: the pen had been found, and Harry's visit had been remembered and logged in her lost property book by the hostess on duty.

So where had Harry Cranworth been and what had he done between lunch-time one day and approximately seven o'clock the next morning? Taxi-drivers could possibly be traced and might help, but that was all, apart from a direct confrontation with Harry. But there was no doubt that the alibi which Harry had concocted for himself—for whatever reason—was shot to pieces; he could have returned home late that evening, killed his wife and departed. But where? This must surely involve someone else. Could it be Steve? And, thought Tansey, it was a curiously amateurish attempt at an alibi, if it were such. No one in their senses in these circumstances would make a point of being so readily identified at the airport at his actual time of return.

But Steve too had lied by supporting Harry's story. He

could be covering for his brother or *vice versa*. Tansey had no doubt that they were close. But how close? Close enough to enter into a conspiracy to murder? And then there was the question of motive.

Tansey gave up temporarily. Except in the unlikely event of a confession by one or other of the brothers—and even a confession might well not be enough to stand up in Court— this was not going to be the simple case that the authorities at the Yard had envisaged when they passed it over to the new man attached from the Thames Valley Force, Tansey thought cynically.

With more care than he had ever taken since he first reached his present rank Detective Chief Inspector Tansey began to draft his report for his superior officers.

Having decided to let Harry and Steve Cranworth stew in their own lies until the following day at least, Dick Tansey didn't stay late at Seymour Place. As he refused the offer of a police car and walked back to his—or rather the Porters'— flat, he wondered how he was going to break the news of Jean Cranworth's death to Hilary. He half-hoped that she might already have heard, but even then her professional interest would have been aroused and she would want to know all the details. If Jean had been a stranger to her he would have been fully prepared to discuss the case with her —he had learnt to value Hilary's opinions—but he was afraid that she might find her old friend's shocking death hard to take.

On the doorstep of the block of flats Tansey met David Horner, an evening paper tucked under his arm. Tansey could just read part of the headline: MURDER IN MAN —He had no need to read more. The media wouldn't have wasted much time.

'Shocking business, this,' Horner said, pointing to the paper before putting his key in the lock. 'But I expect you'll know all about it, Mr Tansey. Are you in charge of the investigation?'

'I'm one of the officers,' Tansey acknowledged curtly in an attempt to forestall further questions. 'But a case of this kind takes the efforts of a great many people,' he added more pleasantly, remembering that the Horners were close neighbours.

As it happened, David Horner had no opportunity to satisfy any curiosity he might have felt. He had unlocked the front door and because it was heavy had gone through it first, holding it open for Tansey to follow. At once there was a loud protest.

'Mr Horner, how many times have I told you—and everyone else in these flats—you shouldn't ever—' A small purple-clad figure appeared from behind David Horner. 'Ah, it's you, Mr Tansey,' said Mrs Meade.

Over the head of the porteress Horner grinned at Tansey. 'Come, Mrs Meade,' he said, 'you can't very well blame me for letting in the police.'

Before she could answer he gave a wave with his hand and bounded up the stairs. Mrs Meade glared after him. Then she turned her attention to Tansey.

'It's too easy to let in a stranger, especially if he looks respectable,' she said. 'I've told everyone time and time again about it. There's too much crime around here these days to take any chances. So, unless you know the person, don't let him—or her—in, Mr Tansey. Shut the door and make them ring. That's a good, safe rule. Your own crime prevention officer told me.'

'I'll remember,' Tansey said meekly.

'And please tell your wife.'

'I will.'

'I wouldn't be surprised if that wasn't how the villain got into that poor girl's place in Manchester Square. What do you think, Mr Tansey?'

What Tansey was thinking at that point was unprintable. Mrs Meade, he had decided, was a menace, and David Horner had shown great initiative in making his successful escape. The Chief Inspector certainly wasn't prepared to answer her question directly, so he resorted to ambiguity. 'I think you're quite right, Mrs Meade. It's sensible to be careful,' he said, edging past her. 'Now, if you'll excuse me.' Emulating Horner, he ran up the stairs.

'Hello, Dick. I'm in here,' Hilary called as soon as she heard him come into the hall.

'Hello, darling.'

Hilary was sitting on a settee knitting busily, and Tansey felt a rush of affection for his wife that made what he had to say to her seem even more loathsome. He had known as soon as she held up her face to be kissed that she didn't know about Jean. He sat down opposite her and tried to smile.

'I've something to tell you, Hilary,' he said. 'Not good news, I'm sorry to say.'

'What?' Intent on her knitting, Hilary was less responsive than he had expected, but when Tansey gave no immediate reply she looked across to him anxiously. 'Dick, they've not gone and put some wretched man over your head in this murder case, have they? I mean the one in Manchester Square? Natalie Smythe told me a girl had been killed there, and I wondered—'

'Hilary, stop! And listen. I'm in charge of the case. That part's fine. Everyone is being very helpful. But—darling— the girl who was murdered was your friend, Jean Cranworth.'

'Jean? Oh no!' Hilary put the knitting down in her lap and stared at it vacantly. Then she recovered from her first shock. 'How did it happen? When? I got the impression from Natalie—she'd been told by her hairdresser—that someone had been walking through the Square late last night and had been mugged and knifed. Admittedly Natalie said she didn't know how accurate the story was, but—but—'

'It wasn't like that at all, Hilary.'

Without going into too many details, Tansey told her what he knew. He hesitated about alerting her not to repeat it to anyone else, and decided that such a warning was unnecessary.

Hilary was continuing to recover, and her training was coming to the fore. She spoke as if she were thinking aloud about a case in which she had no personal interest, almost as if she were making a statement. 'I left Jean yesterday afternoon about three-fifty, because I was back here at four. She said nothing to suggest she was going out later or that she was expecting anyone else, so I may have been the last person—apart from the killer—to see her alive.' She paused, and then added, 'We'd had a good day. We gossiped about old friends and . . .'

Tansey knew better than to interrupt Hilary's train of thought. He realized that she was reviewing her hours with Jean Cranworth from a professional viewpoint. She began to speak again, more slowly and thoughtfully.

'This may or may not help, but I got the impression, though Jean didn't make it explicit, that Harry wasn't always faithful to her, and that he might be in the middle of an affaire which was hurting her a lot. Perhaps I wasn't very sympathetic, because she suddenly pretended she was talking about Steve, not Harry. But I don't believe she was.'

'She didn't suggest that she might have strayed herself, did she? As a kind of retaliation, perhaps?' It was obviously a sensitive issue and Tansey's question was tentative.

But Hilary responded immediately. 'Definitely not. I'm sure she is—was—very much in love with Harry. No, whoever killed her, it wasn't a boyfriend—a lover.' She

shook her head. 'But there's something I don't understand
—what on earth would make her open her door—both
doors; there's one downstairs and another—'

'I know, Hilary,' said Tansey gently.

'Yes, of course. But what would make her open them to
a stranger at that time? She even warned me that the district
wasn't all that safe at night.'

'Perhaps it was a friend—I don't mean a boyfriend—
someone she knew and wouldn't dream of suspecting.'

'Perhaps. It seems more feasible than a man delivering
flowers in the middle of the night—especially as you say
there was no sign of them in the place. But I can't imagine
a motive. Why should anyone want to kill poor Jean?'

'We'll find out,' Tansey said with conviction. 'You go on
with your knitting, darling, while I get us both a drink.
Then we'll have supper.'

'Yes,' said Hilary, and sighed; she didn't feel like eating.
'There's a casserole in the oven.'

CHAPTER 6

Overwhelmed by the almost childish violence of their
mutual anger, the Brooke-Browns had forgotten that their
sitting-room window was open to the morning air, so that
anyone in the mews below who cared to listen could hear
every word they were saying.

Their next-door neighbour, Paul Gainsford, was in the
habit of cleaning his car regularly in the mews outside his
garage, partly for exercise and partly because his nature
was fastidious—and he was one of those who took amused
advantage of this opportunity. He ceased his work and
listened unashamedly. The quarrel was loud and noisy, and
the fishmonger's delivery boy, riding slowly by over the

cobbles on his bicycle, stopped to grin broadly at Gainsford and give him a thumbs-up sign.

'You said it was all over between you,' came Donald's high, rather whining voice from the windows above. 'You promised me, Catherine. You swore it was finished, that you'd told Harry that for my sake you couldn't go on, and he'd accepted the situation. It's not true, is it?'

'Yes, it is! I'm not a liar. How dare you call me a liar!'

'Because that's what you are! But you won't be able to lie to the police, Catherine. Sooner or later they'll be here with their questions—and you'll have to tell them!'

'Tell them what, you damned fool?'

'Tell them you were with Harry Cranworth the night his wife was murdered, of course.'

There was a sudden silence, and when the Brooke-Browns resumed their dialogue they were no longer shouting at each other. It was as if a sudden appreciation of the reality of death—and sudden, intentional murderous death—had quietened their emotions and their voices.

Leaving his car, Paul Gainsford took several surreptitious steps to bring him almost under the Brooke-Browns' window. He was unaware that he presented an almost ludicrous sight. He was a small neat man in his early fifties who had always prided himself on his appearance; an unkind acquaintance had once remarked that his hair and his shoes were invariably so shiny and immaculate that they must be polished with the same brushes. Now, ill-clad in dungarees, with a bucket of water in one hand and a large sponge in the other, he looked as if he had been miscast as a comic window-cleaner.

The pause had ceased and now Catherine was speaking again. 'I was *not* with Harry! I was *not* with Harry!' she was saying, as if the repetition of the incantation gave it greater validity. 'What the hell makes you think I was, Donald?'

'Jean thought you were. She rang up here—and I'm

certain she was checking on you—and Harry. And if you
weren't with Harry, where were you?'

'That's my business.'

'And mine. I'm your husband, remember.'

'Remember! Remember! How could I forget I married a
mouse instead of a man?'

'OK! So I'm a mouse! I've let myself be cuckolded. But
you're a bitch, Catherine, and I'm warning you. You're
going too far. One of these days you'll end up like poor Jean
Cranworth. The only difference'll be that you deserved
it.'

'Don't you threaten me, Donald. You haven't the courage
to put a threat into practice. You're not even a mouse.
You're a bit of mouse's shit!'

There was the sound of a door slamming, and it seemed
likely to Paul Gainsford that Donald had fled and not
heard the end of his wife's vicious diatribe. Wondering that
Catherine Brooke-Brown, whom he considered a snobbish
and pretentious woman, should produce such unexpected
vulgarity even when she was angry, Gainsford moved
quickly. He was well hidden behind his car when, as he had
expected, Donald came bustling out of the house and set off
down the mews as rapidly as he could. There was no sign
of Catherine.

Gainsford finished cleaning his car, though not as
thoroughly as he had intended. His mind wasn't on the job.
He had heard the Brooke-Browns quarrelling before, but
never so savagely as on this occasion, and the apparent
subject of the dispute intrigued him. He himself knew the
Cranworths, though only very casually—he was a senior
partner in a successful firm of architects whose officers were,
by coincidence, in Manchester Square quite close to the
Cranworths' building—and, like everyone in the neighbourhood, he had studied with intense interest what the media
had said about Jean's death. This, he guessed, was largely

surmise; so far the police had not been forthcoming. Now, inevitably, he couldn't help wondering just what truth there was in Donald's accusations, and where Catherine had really been on the night Jean was killed.

He went back into his own house. He had already shaved. He showered, put on a dark suit and an Old Etonian tie that he always hoped would impress his clients.

The next event in his ordered life was breakfast. He lingered over coffee with his wife, Alysia, a plump and comfortable woman about his own age. He was in no hurry. His first appointment was not until eleven-thirty, and he had told his secretary he would be in late. He listened as Alysia spoke of Jean Cranworth's murder, but he didn't mention that he had overheard the Brooke-Browns quarrelling about it. Though she did her best to hide her feelings, his wife, he knew, disliked Catherine Brooke-Brown, and there were some episodes that were better not recalled.

Tansey, accompanied by Sergeant Sester, found Harry and Steve Cranworth still at Manchester Square. The brothers were in Steve's flat, and were just finishing their breakfast when the two police officers arrived.

'I'm glad we caught you,' Tansey said.

Steve stared at the Chief Inspector, as if startled. Then he relaxed. 'Things that might have been better expressed,' he commented. Then he added, 'Seriously, you were lucky. Ten minutes and we'd have been gone, I in the hope of unearthing the next best-seller from the pile of dross on my desk, and Harry to help boost our export trade.'

'I've got to go to my office,' Harry said quickly and somewhat defensively. 'It's important I discuss the business I put through in Paris. Besides, there's nothing I can do here. I've been in touch with Jean's parents and naturally they're upset and—and anxious about the funeral, but what can I tell them? Until the police release the—the—'

Harry didn't complete the sentence, as if he couldn't bring himself to utter the word 'body'. To Tansey both the Cranworths seemed restless, if not downright apprehensive. Steve was cloaking his nervousness with a certain facetiousness, while Harry was fidgeting and over-anxious to make excuses for himself.

Steve said, 'As a matter of fact, Chief Inspector, we're glad you caught us, too. Otherwise—'

He hesitated and, as he did so, Tansey nodded at Sester, who produced two legal-sized documents from the briefcase he was carrying. The Chief Inspector now spoke slowly and carefully, 'These are typed transcripts of the statements you made yesterday. I hope they're accurate. Would you please read them carefully before initialling each page and signing them. I must take this opportunity to remind you of the importance of statements like these. They are legal documents, and could be used as evidence of perjury.'

The Cranworths stared at the papers, and then at each other. Tansey had made sure that they were aware of the menace in his remarks. He knew that their statements were false, and he was determined to make them admit it. As a result of more hard work combined with good luck at least part of Mr Arbuthnot's evidence had been corroborated. A taxi-driver had been traced who had picked up a man with a bag and a briefcase on the Marylebone Road and driven him to the Cranworths' house in Manchester Square on Tuesday morning. The driver remembered the fare for two reasons: it had been his last trip before he went off his night shift, and the gent, apologizing for the short journey, had given him a very generous tip. The passenger had not as yet been formally identified, but it seemed an odds-on bet that it was Harry Cranworth.

Assuming this was so, here was Harry Cranworth once again almost going out of his way to draw attention to his movements, as he appeared to have done in the British

Airways Executive Lounge at Heathrow. This quirk—if
that was an appropriate word—worried Tansey, though for
the moment he was prepared to ignore it.

'Well,' he said when the Cranworths continued to study
their statements but made no effort to sign them. 'Are you
finding a lot of errors?'

'You could say that.' Harry Cranworth grinned sheep-
ishly. 'The fact of the matter is that—that—'

'We were going to tell you,' said Steve. 'We'd like to
revise our statements—make some amendments.'

'What about simply tearing them up?' Tansey demanded.
'You know as well as I do that they're both a pack of lies.
More truthful versions would be a great help—to us, and
probably to you. Surely I don't have to remind you that a
brutal murder's been committed, right here in this house,
just one floor below us. Your wife, Mr Harry Cranworth,
was—'

'Stop! For God's sake, of course you don't need to remind
me. If you think I'll ever forget seeing her—' Harry buried
his face in his hands, and his shoulders shook.

'Chief Inspector!' Steve protested angrily.

It was a good act, Tansey thought, if it were an act. He
wasn't sure. From the first moment he met them he had
instinctively distrusted both the Cranworths, and what he
had learnt of them from Hilary, however second-hand, had
done nothing to change his opinion. But he was a competent
police officer, and he tried not to let this subjective judgement influence him.

Giving them the benefit of the doubt, he said, 'OK.
Everyone makes mistakes. Shall we start again ? But, please,
this time—the truth.'

'It's not exactly a pretty story,' Steve Cranworth began,
'and it may shock you—even in these days.'

'Jean Cranworth's death wasn't exactly pretty, Mr Cranworth,' Tansey said harshly. 'I found that shocking.'

'All right. Then I'll give it to you straight. Harry and I share a girlfriend. And by share, I mean share. On Monday —it's hard to believe it was only two days ago—Harry came back from Paris on the lunch-time flight and went at once to her place. I joined them later in the afternoon, as soon as I could get away from the office. The three of us spent the night together and—how shall I put it?—I assure you a luscious time was had by all.'

'Go on, Mr Cranworth,' Tansey said levelly.

'There's not much more to it. Harry left first in the morning, about seven it must have been, and got a taxi here.'

'Where did you pick up the cab?' Tansey turned to Harry.

'On the Marylebone Road. It was a short ride, but my bag was heavy. The driver might remember me—'

'He does,' said Tansey shortly, thinking it would do no harm to demonstrate that the police probably knew a good deal more than they were admitting.

'Oh,' replied Harry. Then, after a pause, 'Well, when I got in I found Jean.' He shuddered. 'It was awful. I'd expected her to be up, getting early-morning tea—or having a bath or something. I didn't know what to do. She was obviously dead.'

'So what did you do?'

'I went up to Steve's flat and phoned him to come immediately. He was here in—in fifteen minutes.'

'Less than that, Harry. Our girlfriend brought me on her motorbike.'

'She rides a motorcycle?' The question was forced out of Tansey.

'Yes. She says it's the quickest way to get around London —either that or on foot. Anyway, it was obvious we had to call the police, but the problem was what to say. We decided on the story Harry had intended to tell Jean—about getting home late and spending the night in my flat.'

'Why didn't you tell the police the truth in the first place, and save us all a great deal of trouble?'

'Isn't that obvious? Of course, it's what we should have done, but the situation was pretty ghastly. We had visions of headlines in the gutter press. Poor Jean lying here dead, while we were enjoying ourselves. Think what could be made of that. Besides, it wasn't just us. We felt we had to protect our girlfriend.'

'So what made you change your mind?' Tansey asked curiously.

'We decided we'd been foolish.'

'Why was that, Mr Cranworth?'

'Well, we knew we'd acted on the spur of the moment,' said Harry Cranworth. 'Then, thinking it through, even before you produced these formal documents, we realized that when you started to check up on it our story wouldn't hold water. I'm sorry, truly I am, but there you are. We panicked.'

'So you'll sign fresh statements on the lines you've described?' Tansey said and, when the two brothers nodded, 'I assume this—this girlfriend you speak of will confirm all you've told me.'

'Yes,' said Steve with no further comment.

'Right. Then her name, address and—' Tansey thought better of adding occupation.

'Her name—Chief Inspector, I beg of you, please keep it from the media if you possibly can—her name is Gemma Fielding, and she lives—'

There was a minor interruption. Sergeant Sester, who had been taking down in his impeccable shorthand every word that had been uttered dropped his pad and pencil on the floor. They waited a moment while he groped for them, and then Steve Cranworth continued to dictate the address.

*

'You know this Miss Fielding, Sergeant?' said Tansey as they drove back to the Station.

'It depends what you mean by "know", sir. Certainly not as those two claim to know her. But she's well known in this manor—mainly because she's such a strange character. Wears the oddest clothes—long cloaks and harem trousers and things. She kind of flounces round the place expecting attention.' Sester grinned. 'She usually gets it, too.'

The description immediately reminded Tansey of the woman in Madame Sagne's of whom Hilary had spoken. 'Is she a librarian?' he asked doubtfully.

'Yes. She works in the reference department of the Marylebone Public Library.' Sester shook his head. 'I suppose the Cranworths' story must be true—after all, they know we're going to check on it—but I still find it hard to believe. She's always struck me as more the "Don't touch me" type, if you know what I mean, sir.'

Tansey nodded. He would have to talk to Gemma Fielding, but there was no urgency. He accepted Sester's logic. Even if the Cranworths' alibi were false, they would have fixed it with her in advance. And there was something he wanted to do before he interviewed the woman.

When they reached Seymour Street, Tansey looked at the latest reports in the Incident Room, then went to his office and telephoned Hilary. 'Business,' he said briefly. 'Can you remember exactly what Jean said about that exotic woman in the cloak who came into the coffee shop to collect a cake? It could be important,' he added.

'Gemma Fielding. She's a librarian.' Hilary asked no questions. 'Jean said she was Steve Cranworth's current girlfriend, and that he seemed to be pretty smitten because the affaire had lasted some while.'

'And Jean was talking about Steve? Was there any suggestion that Harry was or had been involved with the Fielding woman too?'

'None. I'm sure of it, Dick. Jean seemed to be amused, as if Steve and Gemma would make an odd pair. She wasn't in the least unhappy about it. Her remarks about Harry were much more vague and general. She never named anyone in connection with him—and then she pretended she'd been talking about Steve.'

'I see. Thanks, Hilary. That could be a help. 'Bye for now, darling.'

'Dick!'

'Yes? Have you thought of something else?'

'Between you and me only. I told you that as we were leaving the coffee shop Jean introduced me to a woman called Brooke-Brown—Catherine Brooke-Brown. It could be my imagination—which is why I say keep it between us —but though outwardly Jean and this Catherine were friendly, it seemed to me that they didn't like each other much. Of course, there may be nothing to it, but . . .'

'*But*, indeed. Thank you very much, Sergeant!'

'My pleasure, sir!'

CHAPTER 7

'No! No! Certainly not! What the hell are you suggesting! I shall deny it—you, Harry, everything!'

Gemma Fielding slammed down her telephone receiver with such force that the crack reverberated along the line, and caused Steve Cranworth to wince and rub his ear. He put down his phone more carefully, and turned to his brother.

'You heard, Harry?'

'I could scarcely fail to hear.' Harry Cranworth was bitter. 'In God's name, what are we going to do now? You

were so sure she'd go along with it, Steve. You said it was
a safe bet.'

'I know, I know. I was wrong,' said Steve. 'In the heat
of the moment—when we were talking about possible alibis
—I wasn't thinking straight. Now, on reflection, I can't
blame Gemma for being angry. It must have been a shock
to her to imagine such a version of her private life suddenly
becoming very public. She might have felt differently if she
hadn't been out of London, so that I could have seen her
and talked to her in person, rather than just on the phone.
But, as it is—'

'As it is, we're in deeper than ever,' Harry said angrily.
'Let's face it, this man Tansey's no fool, and like all cops
he'll be eager to break the case. As soon as he's spoken to
Gemma he'll be arresting both of us.'

Steve remained silent and Harry groaned aloud. 'Oh
God, why did I ever listen to you? We've been too clever
by half, Steve. And now I'm afraid we've had it. At least, I
have, though you're involved too, you know. I wonder how
long you get these days for brutally doing away with your
wife. Poor, dear Jean! You might call this her revenge.'

'Don't be a fool, Harry! There's no question of you going
to prison merely because—'

'You know how the police mind works. Means. Opportunity. Motive.' Harry Cranworth spoke sadly. 'As to
means, any moron can make a garrotte. Opportunity? I've
now produced two false alibis, and it would probably have
been simpler for me to kill Jean than for anyone else to
attempt it. So if Tansey finds out that she threatened me—
that I had a motive—'

'How could he? No one knows about that except us.'

'It's possible Jean told her parents—or some friend.'

For a long minute there was silence between the brothers.
Harry went across to the window and stared down at the
dusty shrubs in the Manchester Square garden. He was the

picture of a man in defeat—his expression was grim, his shoulders hunched. Behind him Steve too looked grim, but not defeated; his face, even his stance, suggested purpose and a degree of menace.

'Cheer up, my old Harry,' he said. 'We're not done yet —and we're not going to be done.'

It was late in the morning when Detective Chief Inspector Tansey and Detective-Sergeant Sester arrived at Seymour Street Station. They had been to the village of Durenster, in Hampshire about a hundred miles south-west of London. Jean Cranworth's parents, a Mr and Mrs Totham, had retired there.

The visit had been brief and, from Tansey's point of view, of marginal importance. Mrs Totham had broken down, and been taken upstairs by her sister who was staying with them at this tragic time. Mr Totham, equally upset, hid his grief by an initial display of anger. He was furious with everyone—with the police for not protecting innocent women in their beds; with Harry Cranworth for being in Europe instead of in his right place by his wife; with Steve, who should have been keeping an eye on Jean if Harry had been forced to be away—and especially with the media.

While Sester kept well in the background, Tansey listened patiently, expressing his agreement with all Mr Totham's complaints, even when he slated the local police for not preventing a newspaper reporter from sneaking into the Tothams' house and stealing a photograph of Jean.

'It was one of my favourite pictures of her. She had come to tell us that she'd got engaged to Harry, and she was so happy,' he said sadly as his mood changed. 'I never saw her so happy again, not even at her wedding. Perhaps she was already regretting her decision.'

'Did she regret it, do you think, Mr Totham?' Tansey asked, interested.

'Oh yes. There's no doubt about that. Jean and I were very close, and the last time she was here she told me that Harry was having another affair, and she'd warned him she'd been through enough already—that if he didn't stop she'd divorce him. He promised, of course—'

'Why?'

'Why what?'

'Why should he mind a divorce?'

Mr Totham hesitated. Then: 'I got the impression it was vital the other woman shouldn't be involved. I didn't ask why, and I don't know.' Mr Totham looked meaningfully at the Chief Inspector. 'Anyway, Harry can do what he likes now, can't he? He's free—free of my Jean.'

It was a heavy-handed hint. Clearly Mr Totham disliked Harry Cranworth, and wanted to believe that he was in some way responsible for Jean's death. But Mr Totham wasn't stupid, and he knew that the threat or prospect of divorce, especially when there were no children to consider, was no longer a serious matter—and certainly in itself no motive for murder.

'It's not as if Jean left a lot of money,' he said, as if reading Tansey's thoughts. 'She can't have had more than the few hundred she inherited from an aunt, and if she'd divorced Harry she certainly wouldn't have demanded any from him—she'd have been much too proud. No, I'm sure she'd have gone back to nursery teaching and been independent.'

This view of Jean's life with Harry was perhaps the only new item of information that Tansey was able to obtain from the visit, and it really hadn't required a trip to Durenster. But he wasn't sorry to have met Jean Cranworth's parents; at least he felt he now had a somewhat clearer picture of the victim. But, while he couldn't prevent himself from sharing Mr Totham's dislike of Harry Cranworth—though to a lesser degree—he still found it hard to believe that Harry had killed his wife, even with Steve's connivance.

The two officers had stopped at a pub on the way back from Durenster for some sandwiches and a pint, and as soon as Tansey had called in at the Incident Room, he retreated to his office and started on the reports that had come in. None of them was helpful. There was no joy to be obtained from any of the florists or delivery firms in the immediate neighbourhood, and the search was being widened. The questioning of individuals who lived and worked, or even merely parked their cars regularly, in Manchester Square had yielded nothing new or relevant. Tansey was reading the report of the PM which he had attended the previous day, when Sergeant Sester interrupted him, grinning broadly.

'There's a lady demanding to see you, sir.'

'Demanding?' Tansey queried.

'Yes. She's already thoroughly demoralized the girl at the desk downstairs. Apparently she stormed into the inquiry area, in spite of the notice saying one at a time please, and interrupted some other clients. It's Miss Gemma Fielding, sir. I don't think she's aware we've been trying to locate her.'

'OK. Show her in. Stay with us. And perhaps you'd better find a WPC to be here too.'

As Gemma Fielding swept into his office five minutes later Tansey was thankful that he had been warned about her appearance. Even then he was surprised, though he managed to conceal his feelings. He could accept the black shirt and the black pants that fitted into the black boots, all visible as Miss Fielding flung back her black cloak. He could even accept the orange hair. But he had never before seen such intensely blue eyes.

She was taller than he had expected, too, and the thought

flashed across his mind as he rose to greet her that she was quite strong enough to have killed Jean Cranworth. And, what was more, her determined expression suggested that she was quite capable of such an act if she deemed it necessary

'I've come to make a statement,' she said, flatly and without preamble. She glared around at Sergeant Sester and the uniformed woman constable who had remained in Tansey's office. 'Is this necessary?' she asked. 'My statement is private.'

'Regulations, Miss Fielding,' said Tansey soothingly. 'And it's very good of you to come here.'

She considered him speculatively. 'Chief Inspector,' she said at last. 'I learnt early in life that if I didn't look after myself, nobody else would. And I've adhered to one resolution I made in my teens—that I will *not* be used. That is why I'm here.'

'I'm glad you are, Miss Fielding,' said Tansey equably. 'We've been trying to reach you.'

She nodded her understanding. 'I've been in the country visiting my mother, who's not been well recently. But perhaps I should explain that I work in the local public library. Like other public libraries in the City of Westminster and Marylebone, it's open six days a week for long hours. This means that I work shifts, so that my free time isn't regularly spaced. This week, for example, I was off duty on Tuesday and Wednesday, and early Tuesday morning I rode down—'

'Rode?' queried Tansey.

'Yes, rode. On a motorcycle. I have a fairly powerful Yamaha. In London I prefer to walk, but when this isn't feasible, I use the motorcycle. I find it preferable to a small cheap car, and I can't afford a really expensive vehicle.'

Gemma Fielding was speaking quickly in a low, mellow voice and with total assurance. 'I returned to London this morning. I'm not on duty at the library until later. My telephone was ringing when I reached my flat. It was Steve Cranworth with the request that I should support the story he told you. I do *not* support any such story. I repudiate it wholly and utterly.'

Tansey said, 'You would be prepared to state on oath, Miss Fielding, that neither Harry nor Steve Cranworth were at your flat on Monday night?'

'No, not just like that. I live in a block of mansion flats in Hampstead, and Steve drove up to have supper and stayed until just before midnight. I turned him out then because I wanted an early start before the traffic got bad in the morning.'

'And Harry?'

'I haven't seen Harry for weeks, and after hearing this disgusting story—to which they're trying to make me a party—I never want to see him, or his wretched brother, again. I am not a pervert, and have no intention of being labelled as such in the media. I am unmarried, and I have no wish to marry, but like many people I enjoy sex. So from time to time I take a lover. Steve Cranworth has been my lover for the past year. I have never had any such relationship with Harry. I always avoid married men. Do I make myself clear?'

'Perfectly clear, Miss Fielding. I wish everyone were so explicit.' As Tansey told Hilary that evening, it would have taken a bolder man than he to contradict Gemma Fielding. 'To summarize, you can give Steve Cranworth an alibi for Monday night until shortly before midnight only, and you have no alibi at all to offer Harry Cranworth.'

'That is correct.' For the first time since she had entered the room, Gemma Fielding appeared to hesitate. Then she said, 'I don't like gossip, and in normal circumstances I would keep my mouth shut. But as far as I'm concerned the circumstances are not normal, and I don't feel that I owe the Cranworths anything. On the contrary, in fact. So I would suggest that if Harry is trying to cover for one of his girlfriends—and I must admit it amazes me that he should bother—you might mention the name of Catherine Brooke-Brown to him.'

'Thank you,' said Tansey, amused that the apparently astringent Miss Fielding wasn't above a slice of normal human malevolence—or was it a hope for revenge?

'We're grateful for your help,' he said, and held out his hand to her, gesturing to the WPC to escort her from the office.

'Phew!' exclaimed Sergeant Sester when he was alone with Tansey. 'That was one tough female, sir. On a motorbike, too. But it seems that either Harry or Steve or both could have killed Jean Cranworth.'

'Yes, if the formidable Miss Fielding was telling the truth,' Tansey agreed.

Sergeant Sester regarded him, round-eyed. 'But—but, sir, didn't you believe her?'

'As a matter of fact, I did,' Tansey admitted, 'but I'm still not convinced that a Cranworth is the villain—or a brace of Cranworths, for that matter. They're not fools, and I'd have expected them to be more efficient if they really had planned to kill Harry's wife. Of course they might have argued that was how we'd reason, but any double-bluff like that implies an extraordinary degree of cunning on their part.'

'Besides, when you come to think of it, I suppose there's not much of a motive, sir. As far as I can see, this Harry would have had nothing to lose if his wife had divorced him. You'd think he might have been glad to be free, as her father said.'

'Frankly, I can't imagine anyone having a motive for killing Jean Cranworth—except after raping her,' Tansey said sadly. 'She seems to have been a nice, quiet, long-suffering woman.'

He rose to his feet. 'Ah well, I suppose the next step is to go and talk to Harry again, if he's at home.'

Harry Cranworth was at home—that is, he was in brother Steve's flat, where to judge from the clutter he was now camping. He greeted the police officers without surprise. He looked unkempt and unshaven.

'I know,' he said wearily. 'Gemma Fielding's refused to lie on my behalf. You can't blame her. Steve thought she'd do it for his sake, but he was wrong. In fact, she's thrown the book at him too, poor old Steve.'

'Mr Cranworth, are you drunk?' Tansey asked suddenly as Harry slurred his words.

'Certainly not, Chief Inspector. I had a liquid lunch, but I'm as sober as a—whatever it is.'

'Judge,' Sester said involuntarily.

'That is not the kind of person I wish to consider,' said Harry Cranworth firmly and pompously. 'But I'm being inhospitable. Would either of you gentlemen like a drink?'

'Mr Cranworth, sit down and listen to me.' Tansey's patience had snapped. 'You're in trouble, bad trouble. You and your brother could both go to jail for deliberately obstructing the police during a murder investigation. Do you understand that?'

Harry nodded. 'Yes. We've been stupid.'

'But you've got a chance. Either I warn you formally and we take you down to the Station right now, or you tell us the truth—and I mean the truth, not a third variation of your lies. Which is it to be?'

'They weren't all lies.'

'The truth, Mr Cranworth!'

In fact, what Harry Cranworth now had to say proved little different from his previous statement. He had returned to London at lunch-time on Monday, gone straight to a friend's house—not Gemma Fielding's—and arrived home sometime before seven the following morning to find Jean dead. He had woken Steve, who had left Gemma around midnight.

'And that, Chief Inspector, is the unadulterated truth—but I'm not going to tell you the name of my friend.'

'What about Catherine Brooke-Brown?' Tansey asked.

'Catherine?' For a moment Harry was clearly startled. Then he regained his self-possession. 'It might have been, but again it might not. Anyway, there would be no point in my telling you, because she—whoever she is—would deny it flatly, just like Gemma Fielding. So we'd be no further forward.'

Harry got to his feet, staggering slightly, and went to a liquor cabinet. He poured himself a generous helping of gin, and added a splash of tonic. He held up his glass.

'Here's to you, Chief Inspector—Sergeant! I hope you find whoever killed my Jean—and find him quick. He must be mad, because there can't have been any reason to kill her. So find him, Tansey, before he kills the next woman!'

It was a drunken tirade but, though he found it hard to admit, it worried Dick Tansey.

CHAPTER 8

The inquest on Jean Cranworth was adjourned at the request of the police, though the body was released for burial, and in the week that followed the garrotting of a young woman in Marylebone dropped out of the news—overshadowed in the media by the shooting of two police officers in the City, the disappearance of a ten-year-old girl in Hampstead and a major train crash.

But Jean Cranworth was far from forgotten in Seymour

Street, and even in some unexpected locations it continued to be a matter of interest. Naturally among the Tanseys' neighbours it had signally failed to lose its value as a subject for inquiry and a topic of conversation.

Inevitably Hilary, who was at home or shopping in the area during the day, bore the brunt of local curiosity. Temporarily cut off from a personal involvement with police investigation—work which had absorbed her interest—she had a certain amount of sympathy with the probers, but the fact that she had to respect her husband's confidences made her cautious. In particular, she found Grace Horner trying; sometimes it seemed to Hilary that Mrs Horner listened for signs of life from the Tanseys' flat in order to come into the hall and waylay her.

'Oh, my dear,' she would say brightly, perhaps catching Hilary as she attempted to open her front door silently and take in her milk without being seen. 'How are you? And are there any developments?'

But one morning the theme changed, 'My dear, what good news! Thanks to that clever husband of yours, I'm sure. You must be pleased.'

'Mrs Horner, I'm sorry, but I've no idea what you're talking about,' Hilary said firmly.

'But of course you have. You must be teasing me. It's in the morning paper. It says there's been a breakthrough in the Manchester Square murder case—a witness has come forward, and the police expect to make an arrest in the near future.'

'That's splendid,' said Hilary, who in the course of her career had heard many such forecasts based on nothing except the imagination of a reporter with space to fill. 'Let's hope it's true.'

'You mean your husband didn't tell you?' Mrs Horner was obviously incredulous. 'Well, well! Anyway, I'm off to the hairdresser's at nine and the girls there usually know the latest news. The customers love to gossip. What about coming in to have a coffee with me when I get back?'

'That's very kind of you, Mrs Horner, but I'm afraid I can't. I'm expecting a friend for coffee myself.'

'Oh, I see.' Mrs Horner waited hopefully for an invitation to join them, but when none came she smiled bravely, patted her hair and declared, 'Then I'll say goodbye for now, dear.'

'Goodbye, Mrs Horner.'

Thankfully Hilary closed her front door, avoiding the temptation to slam it. It was a pity, she thought, that there was no truth in Mrs Horner's suggestion of a breakthrough in the Manchester Square case. In fact, the investigation seemed to have reached a position of stalemate, and Dick was depressed. The list of possible suspects remained short —there were only two names on it, to be exact: Harry and Steve Cranworth. The main difficulty was that the crime appeared to have been motiveless. There was no question of an arrest at present, or indeed in the foreseeable future.

Sighing, Hilary went about her business, washing up the breakfast, making the bed, dusting the flat and preparing a coffee tray ready for Natalie Smythe when she put in an appearance later. Hilary did these chores automatically, her mind on the next day and Jean Cranworth's funeral. She and Dick had almost quarrelled about the funeral, she recalled ruefully.

He had arrived home late the evening before in a foul temper. 'I was just about to leave the office when the phone went,' he said. 'I was tempted to leave it, but I knew they'd get me somehow. And you'll never guess who it was—that bloody Minister, Hector Greyling.'

'What on earth did he want? There haven't been any more footprints on his flowerbed, have there?'

'No, but it's the same general idea—the safety of his beloved wife. It seems he's just taken in the fact that a helpless woman was attacked in her own home, comparatively close by, and killed in an appalling fashion. The Manchester Square murder evidently didn't make the foreign press, or he missed the item in between his meetings and his diplomatic receptions. Anyway, now he's got it into his thick head that whoever killed Jean was a maniac, and will automatically be after his Pamela next.'

'There's been nothing to suggest such a thing, has there?'

'Apparently there was a call to her private phone line. Greyling answered it himself, and gave the number. The caller then immediately put down his receiver. Otherwise, there's not a shred of evidence. In fact, with their security precautions, the servants and a police patrol she must be one of the least vulnerable women in London.'

'Unless she invites the killer in. After all, it seems that Jean did just that.'

'Why the hell would she?' Tansey was exasperated. 'Still, nothing would satisfy Greyling except that I went round there and told him every detail of the case so that he could warn his wife and the staff, and put them on their guard.'

'Did you have to go, Dick?'

'Go? Yes. A mere Chief Inspector doesn't refuse a Minister of the Crown. And I told him some of the more unpleasant details, but really nothing he couldn't have learnt from the media. When I left him he was all for getting on to the Diplomatic Protection Group at the Yard!'

'If he's so scared, why doesn't he make his wife go into the country?'

'Evidently that's not practical at the moment. They've a lot of public and private engagements, and her presence is needed in London.'

'Ah, public engagements. That reminds me, Dick, about Jean's funeral. Do you think it matters that I haven't got a hat? The Tothams are a bit old-fashioned and—'

And that was when the altercation had begun.

It had never occurred to Hilary that she wouldn't go to

Jean's funeral, even though it was to take place at Durenster. Jean had been a very old friend and, though she herself had scarcely seen the Tothams since she left home, her parents had kept in touch. They would certainly be at the funeral, and they would expect her to be there too, as would the Tothams.

Dick, however, had other ideas. He had intended to go to the funeral himself, with Sergeant Sester. Their police presence would be a mark of respect, and a gathering of Jean's friends and relations could conceivably show up something of interest. But on his previous visit to Durenster, he had not mentioned the relationship between his wife and their murdered daughter. Why should he? But if both the Tanseys went to the funeral the connection would be unavoidable. They could hardly pretend to be strangers when Hilary's parents would be there, and the situation would be highly embarrassing.

If Tansey had been less frustrated by his failure to make progress with the case, and he had not been further irritated by Hector Greyling's ridiculous fears, he might have been more sympathetic towards Hilary. As it was, they had come dangerously close to a real dispute, Hilary thought sadly, thankful that in the end it had been averted.

Natalie Smythe arrived promptly at eleven, carrying three hats, any of which she was prepared to lend to Hilary for Jean's funeral. They went into the bedroom, and Hilary tried them on, eventually deciding on a black velvet beret.

'This will go splendidly with my dark grey suit,' she said. 'Are you sure you don't mind?'

'Of course not. I'm only sorry it was your friend who was killed. I had no idea.'

'How could you? And I've not told anyone but you,' Hilary said quickly.

'Don't worry. I can keep things to myself. You say the

funeral's in the country. How are you going to get there?'

'It's at a place called Durenster in Hampshire, but a friend's driving me.'

Hilary did not explain that her driver would be Detective-Sergeant Sester. The Chief Superintendent at Delta Mike Division, Peter Wilson, had solved the Tanseys' problem. Hilary would go to Jean Cranworth's funeral without her husband, officially as Jean's friend and unofficially as Sergeant Hilary Greenway. Sester would accompany her, but would stay well in the background. If anything of interest were to be revealed, their reports should be adequate. In the circumstances, it was an ideal compromise.

'Let's go and have our coffee,' said Hilary, changing the subject and leading her guest into the sitting-room.

While she was pouring, Natalie Smythe went to the window. 'Here's Mrs Horner,' she said, 'looking as immaculate as ever. I can't think how she does it. She's always so beautifully dressed, with not a hair out of place or a smudged eyebrow. She puts me to shame.'

'Me, too. But don't let her see you or she'll be inviting herself to join us.' Hilary laughed.

'I know what you mean. She can be something of a pest, but she's a kind woman. When I had a bug last winter she shopped for me and brought me little casseroles, and generally looked after me. I can't think what I'd have done without her.'

'That was kind of her.'

Natalie tucked her long legs under her. 'Of course she spoils her son David endlessly. She believes the sun only rises for his benefit. Wretched man!'

'You don't like him?'

'No. He's got clammy hands.'

'That's hardly his fault.'

'Maybe not. But he should keep them to himself. Once he made a pass at me, and it annoyed me. Why men should

imagine that any unmarried woman is fair game, especially
if she's an actress, God knows. Visions of casting couches,
perhaps. Anyway, it wasn't very serious, and I discouraged
him quite readily.'

In her turn, she changed the subject. She expected to be
offered a good part in a play being put on in one of the
suburban theatres, but was having doubts about accepting
it. 'I must be getting old,' she said, 'but the idea of coming
home late at night by myself doesn't appeal to me any more.
It's silly, of course. After all, your poor friend wasn't safe
even in her own house, was she?'

The following morning Hilary left the flat shortly before
nine. Tansey had already gone to work. It was a dull, grey
day, damp and threatening to rain—a suitable day for a
funeral, Hilary thought. Self-conscious in Natalie Smythe's
black velvet beret, she had hoped not to meet anyone, but
Mrs Meade was busy cleaning the entrance hall and it was
impossible to avoid her.

'Good morning, Mrs Tansey. That arrest the papers
promised us in the Manchester Square murder hasn't happened yet, has it? Will it be soon now?'

'I've no idea, Mrs Meade.'

Hilary stepped carefully over the lead to the vacuum
cleaner, and reached the front door. As she opened it a blast
of cold air greeted her. She shivered. Her only raincoat was
a bright yellow PVC garment, which she had decided it was
impossible to wear. To forestall more questions from Mrs
Meade she hurriedly said goodbye, and fled.

Sergeant Sester was waiting for her as arranged at the
corner of Baker Street. In a thick navy blue suit and with a
waistcoat, white shirt and black tie he was both suitably
dressed and comfortably warm. Seeing Hilary's thin clothes
he immediately turned up the car's heater. It was a gesture
she appreciated.

'From one sergeant to another, thanks,' she said, smiling.

Sester grinned at her. 'My pleasure,' he replied.

This exchange set the atmosphere for a pleasant, friendly drive, during which by common consent they both avoided the topic of Jean Cranworth's murder, and spent the time discussing the differences between the Met and the Thames Valley Force. Sester dropped Hilary a short distance from Durenster's village church, and she was lucky enough to meet her parents walking from their car. She had telephoned them, so that they were not surprised to see her.

'Hello, darling,' said her mother. 'Dick not with you?'

'No. He thought it tactful not to come. His sergeant drove me down.'

'A sad day, my dear, said Hilary's father, 'but—but surely not sad enough to warrant that hat. I scarcely recognized you. It's worse than your mother's.'

'I borrowed it.'

Hilary laughed. She was fond of both her parents, but it was her father who usually understood her moods. Together they went into the church, involuntarily pausing for a moment at the sight of the coffin on its trestles in the sactuary before the altar, until they were directed to a pew some way behind the Tothams. From their backs Hilary recognized Mr and Mrs Totham and Jean's brother, Brian, with individuals whom she presumed were his wife and children. Other relations and friends were scattered in the pews further back, and across the aisle in the front pew sat Harry Cranworth, Jean's husband, and his brother Steve. There was no one else sitting with the Cranworths, or for several pews behind.

Instinctively Hilary felt that there was something awry about this arrangement. Harry should have been sitting with the Tothams, not so obviously isolated alone with Steve. She turned around to see if she could spot Sergeant Sester, and was startled to find herself staring directly at Catherine Brooke-Brown, who was wearing a small white hat; only its short black veil made it more suitable for a funeral than a wedding.

The entry of the choir, followed by the officiating clergy-man, and the traditional words which began the service, prevented further research on Hilary's part. Hilary sang the hymns, knelt in prayer and listened attentively to the brief eulogy, but she was curiously unmoved. It was not until the coffin was being lowered into the wet ground that she had trouble containing her tears.

The whole ceremony had lasted less than an hour and Hilary, though she was glad she had come, was thinking that it would have been a waste of her husband's time, when by chance she witnessed a small but unpleasant incident.

The Tothams had invited their relations and a few of their friends who had come from a distance—including Hilary and her parents—to return to their house for a light buffet before setting off on their respective return journeys. Apparently Harry Cranworth had assumed that he and his brother would be included in the invitation, but Mr Totham had other ideas. Hilary, who had been making sure that Sergeant Sester would get some lunch, came on the three men unexpectedly.

'—not having you in my house, Cranworth. Never again. In fact, I sincerely hope never to see you again. You were a rotten husband to my Jean, and now you've got what you wanted. You're free of Jean and, what's more, you're free of her threat to show up that bitch you're sleeping with—'

Mr Totham stopped abruptly as he saw Hilary, but Harry and Steve had already turned away silently. Mr Totham, tears in his eyes, shook his head sadly at Hilary, and stumbled towards the house. She followed more slowly, wondering if she had come upon a new motive for killing Jean—not the threat of divorce, which was hardly credible, but the prospect that the name of Harry's current mistress would be exposed. Yet as she watched a small white hat join the Cranworths in the distance, she found this hard to countenance. After all, innumerable people, from the highest to the lowest in the land, were committing adultery or seeking divorces daily.

CHAPTER 9

Donald Brooke-Brown had followed in his father's and grandfather's footsteps by becoming a Mason, and membership of his Lodge was particularly important to him, for it was the one part of his life that he had managed to protect and keep apart from Catherine. In deference to her views and her constant silly jokes about men wearing aprons and dressing up to live out their fantasies and dabble in black magic, he kept his secret paraphernalia in its wooden case at the premises of his Lodge, safe from his wife's prying eyes, but he resolutely refused to accept any social invitations if they conflicted with his Masonic commitments. He was indeed a dedicated member of the order and, except for the occasional bout of ill-health, never missed a Masonic function.

The Tuesday after the funeral of Jean Cranworth was one of his regular Lodge nights, so Donald dressed himself with more than usual care and said good night to his wife. Catherine herself had decided not to go out that evening; she thought she might be suffering from the early symptoms of a cold.

Next door, the Gainsfords watched television until Alysia decided that she would like to go to bed. She was half asleep when she heard the front door slam and registered that Paul would be putting the cat out. By the time he came upstairs, she was in the middle of a vivid dream. She had no idea of the hour.

It was some while after eleven when the Brooke-Browns'
doorbell rang. Catherine, like most of the neighbours who
were not out for the evening, was already in bed, though
she was still reading. Her first thought was that Donald had
forgotten his keys—an event almost unprecedented—but
then she looked at her bedside clock and realized that it was
too soon for him to return. She thought of ignoring the bell
but it rang again, insistently. At last, irritated, Catherine
got out of bed, put on a robe and went to the window.

The mews was poorly lit and the angle from which she
was peering out at the front door was acute. She could see
little until she opened the window and poked her head out.
Now she could make out what was happening. A man in a
dark leather jacket and a motorcycle helmet was about to
ring the bell for the third time.

'What is it?' Catherine called. 'What do you want?'

There was a perceptible pause before the man inquired,
quite quietly, 'Mrs Brooke-Brown?'

'Yes. I'm Mrs Brooke-Brown.'

'I've got a delivery for you, madam. I'm terribly sorry to
be so late, but it was sent to the wrong address.'

'I'm not expecting any delivery.'

'It's flowers, madam. For Mrs Donald Brooke-Brown.'

Catherine hesitated. Probably nothing but flowers would
have tempted her. But she could guess who had sent them,
and she wanted to read and hold the message that must
accompany them.

'All right. I'll be down in a minute.'

Without a thought for caution, her mind riveted on the
flowers her lover had sent her, Catherine Brooke-Brown
ran downstairs and opened the front door. Just as Jean
Cranworth had done, she instinctively stepped backwards
as the box was thrust at her. Then the killer was in the
house, the front door shut, and a gun pointed at her.

'Turn around! Walk upstairs—slowly!'

Catherine obeyed, but she felt none of Jean's hopelessness or resignation. Naturally, she was fully aware of her immediate danger. She knew what was about to happen—unless she could make an effort to save herself. Promises, bribes, appeals for mercy—none of these would serve. She would have one chance, a physical chance, and one chance only.

As in most mews houses, the staircase was steep and narrow. Almost at the top there was a half-landing and then three more steps at right-angles to the earlier stairs.

Catherine didn't lack courage, and once she had decided on her course of action—her only course of action—she didn't hesitate. As she reached the top of the main flight of stairs she kicked back with all her strength. There was a grunt and a muffled curse and for a moment she thought that her attack had succeeded. But she had forgotten that she was wearing only soft bedroom slippers. Though the man behind her staggered, he didn't fall.

Nevertheless, Catherine ran. Her objective was a small cloakroom with a window facing the mews, and it was almost within reach. If she could get there, bolt the door behind her and then scream out of the window, someone might hear. At least the intruder might be scared and run from the house, leaving her shaken but blissfully unharmed.

It was a happy dream, but it was only a dream. She stumbled over her long robe as she came to the end of the three topmost steps, and to her horror she fell. He was on her at once. She felt the touch of the wire round her neck, and that was the last thing she did feel. She died as her scream was choked off.

The killer hurried. After the care he had taken to make certain his victim would be at home alone, he had been shaken by her sudden attack, and by his narrow escape. He could so easily have fallen headlong to the ground floor and broken a leg, or worse.

He picked up Catherine's slight body, carried her into the bedroom and arranged her as he liked. Then he collected his box of dead flowers and put it in the black plastic bag he produced, neatly folded, from a pocket of his jacket. Pistol ready to hand, he prepared to leave.

As far as he knew, no one had seen him come, and no one saw him go. He walked to the end of the mews, keeping to the shadows as far as possible. There were several lighted windows, but the curtains were all drawn. No one was about, and there was no indication that anyone had paid any attention to the conversation through the window; he had hesitated before calling up to the Brooke-Brown woman in the quiet mews. However, all seemed to be well. His motorbike was where he had parked it. He pushed it out of the mews before mounting it and riding off.

It was but a short distance to the lock-up garage where he kept his car. He stripped off his motorcycle gear, and locked it carefully in the boot with the gun and the plastic bag. The bike, which he had stolen a month ago and hardly used, he placed against the back wall of the garage, and covered with a tarpaulin. His night's work had been ac-complished satisfactorily.

A little more than two hours later—soon after one o'clock the next morning—a taxi drove into the mews and deposited Donald Brooke-Brown in front of his house. He opened the front door carefully and closed it quietly behind him.

It was only minutes before he appeared again. He lurched into the roadway. He attempted to give a cry, but it emerged from his mouth as a croak. Then he vomited into the gutter and, staggering to the Gainsfords' house, he put his thumb on their bell, and with his other hand pounded on their door. A light came on almost at once, a window opened and Paul Gainsford thrust out his head.

'What the hell's going on? Stop making that noise!'

'Paul, it's me, Donald. For God's sake come. Please come!'

Gainsford responded at once. 'Hang on. I'll be with you in a moment.'

Alysia had already been awakened and, as he scrambled into a dressing gown, he said, 'It's Donald. He sounds frantic, God knows what he wants.'

'All right. I'll come too. I'll be down in a minute,' his wife said, preparing to get out of bed. 'It may be Catherine. She could be ill.'

Gainsford opened his front door, and Brooke-Brown nearly fell into the hall. Gainsford had to half carry him into the kitchen, where he sat him at the table.

'Catherine! Oh, Catherine!' Brooke-Brown groaned.

'What about Catherine?' Gainsford asked briskly.

'Catherine—' Brooke-Brown was practically incoherent. 'Catherine's dead. I've just found her. There's a—a wire round her neck—just like—'

'What?'

'Oh my God, no!' Alysia had just come into the kitchen and heard the last sentences.

The Gainsfords exchanged glances. Donald had buried his face in his hands. Clearly he was in no fit state to take any immediate action. Automatically Alysia opened the cupboard where they kept the brandy.

'You'd better go, Paul. But be careful. Remember Manchester Square.'

'Will you be all right?'

She laughed, but she was touched by his solicitude. 'With Donald? Don't be silly, Paul.'

Paul saw her hand on the brandy bottle. 'Not brandy for shock,' he said. 'Hot, sweet tea, isn't it?' Then he went quickly, but still somewhat reluctantly. Incongruously the thought occurred to him that if anyone saw him dodging from one house to the next in his dressing-gown they would think the worst. But the supposed 'worst' would pale into insignificance beside the reality of Catherine Brooke-Brown sharing her bed with a garrotte. He shivered as he went into the next house and up the stairs.

He spent the minimum of time in the bedroom, and didn't linger in the house. Immediately he came into his own kitchen Alysia knew from the brief nod he gave that Donald had told the truth: Catherine was dead—murdered. They both turned to Brooke-Brown, who seemed to be in a daze.

'Dear God!' said Alysia. 'Was it—was it just like that poor girl Jean Cranworth?'

'Yes,' said Paul shortly. 'I must phone the police. Then I'll go and dress. I doubt if any of us'll get any more sleep tonight. All right? I shan't be long.'

By the time Paul returned Donald seemed to have got over the worst of his shock, and was sipping at a mug of tea. He regarded Paul with a tear-stained face.

'I didn't do it,' he said at once. 'I didn't kill Catherine. She wasn't faithful to me. She had lovers, but I didn't kill her. You—'

Gainsford interrupted him, perhaps a shade too quickly. 'Take it easy, Donald. The police are on their way. They'll have a lot of questions for you, so try and get your thoughts straight. Alysia, you go and dress, dear.'

'Yes, I will. You help yourself to a drink—and give him one if you think it's wise. Or tea.' She smiled at her husband comfortingly. 'I made enough for a regiment.'

Dick and Hilary Tansey had gone to bed early. They had made love, not passionately because of Hilary's pregnancy, but quietly and with great enjoyment and devotion. Afterwards they had chatted for a while, about themselves, their return to Oxford, the new house they planned to buy. They didn't mention Jean Cranworth, or any subject remotely connected with Dick's duties.

They were both asleep when the telephone on the bedside table next to Tansey began to trill. After long years of practice at answering such calls he was instantly awake, his mind at once alert. Hilary surfaced more slowly. But she too was fully awake by the time the brief call was over.

'What is it, Dick?' She switched on her bedside lamp.

'Another killing,' he said briefly. 'A garrotting again. It sounds identical to Jean's.'

'Oh no, darling.'

It was a meaningless protest; Hilary was thinking of him rather than anyone else. Tansey ignored her. He was already hurrying into the bathroom. She heard the flush of the lavatory, then water—it would be cold water, she guessed —running in the basin. Tansey had shaved before he came to bed, so he had no need to use a razor, and almost at once he was back and getting into his clothes.

'They said a car was on its way,' he said, struggling into a sweater. 'That means five to ten minutes at this time of night. Try to get some more sleep when I've gone, Hilary.'

'Yes, all right. Dick, who is it? It's not that Minister's wife, is it? Pamela—Pamela Greyling?'

Tansey stopped, one leg in and one leg out of his slacks. 'No. What makes you think it might have been?'

'Only that her husband was so afraid for her.'

'Indeed he was.' Tansey finished dressing. 'But he need not have been. The victim this time was Mrs Brooke-Brown, Catherine Brooke-Brown.'

'Then there could be some connection with Jean,' Hilary said at once.

'Possibly.'

A car hooted quietly in the road outside. Dick Tansey went to the window and moved the curtain as a signal that he was on his way. He bent over and kissed Hilary on the mouth.

'Goodbye, darling. I'll try to phone you during the day if I get the chance.'

''Bye, Dick. Take care.'

Hilary listened to the quiet shutting of the front door and imagined Tansey running down the stairs, letting himself out of the building and getting into the police car. She wondered if the driver was Sergeant Sester. Whoever it was, she wished she could have taken his place.

CHAPTER 10

Detective Chief Inspector Dick Tansey's first impression had been correct. Except for a slightly different setting, the killing of Catherine Brooke-Brown seemed to be a carbon copy of Jean Cranworth's murder.

As in the Manchester Square case, there was no sign of a forced entry into the mews house. The killer either had had a key, or had been willingly admitted by Catherine, who must have opened the door to him. She had been garrotted near the top of the stairs and carried into the bedroom. Her robe had been torn, but she had not been sexually molested in any way. Although Donald Brooke-Brown had so far been unable to make any kind of assessment, there were no indications of a search or signs that anything had been stolen. On the face of it, this was another senseless, purposeless murder.

'D'you think we're dealing with some nut, sir?' asked the inspector in charge of the scene of crime team.

'No!' Tansey spoke definitely. The inspector looked at his superior inquiringly, but Tansey didn't elaborate. In fact, he would have been hard put to explain his certainty that these murders had a logical explanation.

In spite of continuing investigation, no further progress

had been made towards an arrest in the Cranworth case, but suspicion still lay heavy on the brothers, Harry and Steve. The crime, though perhaps unnecessarily theatrical, otherwise had all the hallmarks of a simple domestic affair.

This second murder, at least in Tansey's opinion, added another dimension of intricacy and implied the existence of complications. These he welcomed, for he maintained that the more complex a case appeared on the surface the more likely it was that a solution would be reached. But at the back of his mind he was worried. Hilary's assumption that the dead woman was Pamela Greyling had forced him to wonder if this was to be the last of these homicides.

Having inspected the body and gone through the standard routines, Tansey was glad to escape next door with Sergeant Sester and a uniformed constable. The Brooke-Browns' house was crowded with experts, collecting evidence for other experts. Almost certainly, at some later stage he would be thankful for their work, but at the moment his first objective was to meet those who had been immediately involved in the discovery of the body.

Paul Gainsford opened the door to the officers, and immediately introduced himself. He showed them into a room at the front of the house which was used as a dining-room.

'I'll fetch Donald Brooke-Brown,' he said. 'He's in the kitchen. He was shocked, and we've been giving him tea.'

'I understand he found the body,' said Tansey.

'That's right. The first we knew about it was when he rang our doorbell and banged on our door.'

Tansey nodded. 'Well, suppose you tell me what happened after that, Mr Gainsford, please. Obviously you and your wife are neighbours of the Brooke-Browns—and friends of theirs?'

'Casual friends, yes, and as you say neighbours. It was only natural that when Donald returned to find his wife so

—so brutally killed that he'd turn to us, and of course we were glad to give what help we could.'

'Of course,' Tansey echoed smoothly. His tone caused Sester to bite his lower lip and stifle a grin. 'Now, you were asleep when Mr Brooke-Brown arrived back? You didn't actually hear him until he roused you? Is that right?'

'Yes. My wife and I were both fast asleep in our bedroom upstairs, but when I went to the window and saw who it was I hurried down at once. Donald was practically hysterical—' Paul Gainsford told his story clearly and succinctly. In reality, there was little to tell.

'I see,' said Tansey finally. 'Now we should like to talk to Mr Brooke-Brown. They got on well together, he and his wife, did they?' Tansey made this sound like an unimportant throwaway question.

Gainsford had stood up, believing the interview was over. Now he hesitated, uncertain as to how he should answer. Sester said afterwards that you could almost hear his mind considering his options.

At last Gainsford replied. 'I wish you hadn't asked me that, Chief Inspector. I would prefer to say that all married couples have an occasional spat and leave it there, but—'

'Go on, Mr Gainsford, please.'

'I don't suppose it's in the least relevant, but the other morning I was cleaning my car—'

'Thank you. I'm most grateful,' said Tansey when Gainsford had completed an expurgated account of the row between the Brooke-Browns that he had overheard. 'As you say, it's probably irrelevant, but it's always best to hold nothing back—especially in a serious case like a murder inquiry.' He let Paul Gainsford reach the door of the dining-room. 'By the way, I never asked you. Were you at home the entire evening, until Mr Brooke-Brown roused you?'

Gainsford let his hand fall from the doorknob, and he took a minute to answer. Again, as Sester said, you could hear the wheels whirring. 'As a matter of fact, no,' he said at length. 'I went for a short walk at the time I put the cat out before going to bed. I needed some air. It must have been not long after eleven when I got back.'

'You can't be more precise than that?'

'No, I'm afraid not.' Gainsford laughed. 'Our cat was scratching at the front door when I returned, but there was no one else in the mews.'

'Thank you, Mr Gainsford. Thank you. You've been very helpful.' Tansey turned to Sester. 'On second thoughts I'd like a word with your wife before I see Mr Brooke-Brown. Ask Mrs Gainsford if she'll come in, will you, Sergeant?'

Gainsford's neat features were incapable of showing strong emotion, but momentarily he looked as if he had been beset by a bad smell.

'My wife?' he said. 'You want to question my wife?'

'Naturally,' said Tansey. 'You don't object, do you? You can stay, if you like. Or we can find a woman police officer to join us.'

Gainsford protested no further. He merely showed his tidy white teeth in a dubious smile and said, 'Oh, that won't be necessary, Chief Inspector. I'll help to keep an eye on Donald while you're talking to Alysia.'

Tansey nodded to Sergeant Sester, who leapt to attention. 'Yes, sir!' he said. 'Mrs Gainsford.'

Alysia Gainsford made a more agreeable first impression on Tansey than her husband had done. She showed mild surprise when informed that Donald had gone for such a late walk; she hadn't known about this. Otherwise she confirmed everything he had said. The Brooke-Browns had been casual friends. She and Catherine hadn't much in common. Their interests were quite different. For example, Alysia liked to visit her daughter who lived not far away with her husband and a new baby—the Gainsfords' first grandchild—and she always tried to be home by the time Paul returned from his architect's office. Catherine, she was sure, had led a much more exciting life.

'A little venom mixed with the lady's honey, sir?' commented Sergeant Sester, having seen her from the room and returned. 'Perhaps husband Paul cast an eye in fair Catherine's direction and Mrs G. didn't like it.'

'Catherine was dark,' Tansey remarked. 'And where's Brooke-Brown? You were meant to be fetching him next.'

'He's in the toilet, sir, with a police officer outside. I expect the shock's reached his digestion. He'll be with us as soon as possible.'

Tansey grunted. He was feeling tired, and he wished that Sester wouldn't be quite so ebullient.

At that moment there was a knock at the door of the Gainsfords' living-room, and Donald Brooke-Brown came in.

'Our condolences, Mr Brooke-Brown,' began Tansey. 'This is a great tragedy for you.'

'It's—it's ghastly! My dear Catherine! I loved her so much. I don't know what I shall do without her.' Brooke-Brown mouthed these platitudes earnestly. 'And it was my fault. If only I'd been here. I shall always blame myself.'

'So where were you, Mr Brooke-Brown?'

'Don't you know? It was my Masonic Lodge night. That was the one time I would go off on my own and leave Catherine, though she'd often—' He stopped abruptly, but what he had intended to say in the rest of the sentence was reasonably obvious.

'And who would know you had this regular engagement?' asked Tansey.

Brooke-Brown shrugged. 'Anyone. Any of our friends or acquaintances. Anyone who wanted to know. There's no secret about the dates and places of Masonic meetings, in spite of what you read sometimes.'

'I see,' said Tansey. 'I'm told you rang the Gainsfords' bell soon after one, which means that you arrived home a few minutes earlier. How far away is this Lodge?'

'Er—just the other side of Regent Street—a few minutes in a taxi.'

'And do these meetings usually last so long—into the small hours?'

Brooke-Brown hesitated. At last he said, 'No, they don't. You'll be able to check with other members. Tonight's ended soon after eleven.'

'So—'

'So what was I doing? I wasn't feeling too well, so I went for a long walk. I had a lot to think about. I stopped in a pub off Fleet Street for a drink, though I doubt if anyone will remember me. You know what Fleet Street pubs used to be like when the papers had gone to bed.'

Brooke-Brown paused, and then buried his head in his hands. 'If only I'd known!' he exclaimed. 'My poor, dear Catherine!' Two maudlin tears rolled down his cheek.

Tansey ignored them. 'Don't you think your story's a bit odd, Mr Brooke-Brown?'

Brooke-Brown stared at the Chief Inspector. 'No. No, why should I?'

'You expect us to believe that last night when you weren't feeling well—because you weren't feeling well—instead of coming straight home you went for a two-hour walk that didn't end till early this morning. Well, we shall need details of the Lodge meeting and your fellow-Masons, the names of anyone you met afterwards, the pub you say you visited. All this information will be checked in detail.'

'I know my Lodge and the members, but I didn't meet anyone and, as I said, I doubt if anyone will remember me in the pub. Oh God! Why are you putting me through this now? I need—'

'Quite, sir.' Sergeant Sester seized Brooke-Brown by the

elbow as he half rose from his chair, and ran him from the room.

'That was a convenient moment for him,' Tansey said sourly when Sester returned.

'A perfectly genuine call though, I assure you, sir,' said Sester. 'The constable and I got him there just in time.'

Tansey sighed. 'Well, we'll still have to get all the details he can remember, or is prepared to recall, and start checking. But for now we'll change tack.'

And when a pathetic, white-faced Donald Brooke-Brown returned, Tansey said, 'Your house is very attractive, Mr Brooke-Brown, and worth a lot of money these days. Is it in your name or your wife's, or both of you?'

'My wife's. It was a wedding present—to her—from her father. But what's that got—'

Brooke-Brown's mind must have been turning over very slowly, because it seemed to require a great effort on his part to grasp the purport of Tansey's question. For a long moment he stared into space, his mouth slightly open like an imbecile's, then surprisingly he smiled.

'Yes,' he said. 'It's Catherine's house, Catherine's Jaguar, Catherine's cottage in the country, Catherine's almost everything. Her father was a rich man, and she was the only child. But you've got it wrong, Chief Inspector. I'd have married her if she'd not had a penny. I—I loved her, more than anything in the world. Perhaps she wasn't the most faithful of wives, but I'd never have wanted anyone else.'

His mouth fell open again, and once more he stared into the distance, but this time his words had carried conviction. Donald Brooke-Brown had been devoted to his wife. But that fact, Tansey knew, didn't mean he hadn't killed her. Her admitted infidelities might have driven him over the edge and, doormat though he appeared, he could finally have revolted. It wouldn't be the first time that such a course of events had taken place.

'How well do you know the Cranworths, who live in Manchester Square, Mr Brooke-Brown?' Tansey said.

'Why do you ask that?' Brooke-Brown was abrupt; the question had apparently startled him from his semi-trance.

'You must have realized by now that Jean, Harry Cranworth's wife, was killed in the same way as your own wife.'

'I read the papers.'

'Exactly. And when you know anyone involved in a story, you're more interested.'

'I scarcely knew her. They came to dinner once a while ago and we went there. That's about all.'

'But your wife and Harry Cranworth were quite close friends, shall we say?'

'So what?' said Brooke-Brown desperately. 'Catherine had lots of—friends.'

'Come on, Mr Brooke-Brown. Let's face facts,' said Tansey brutally. 'Doesn't it seem likely that someone who, whatever his normal relations with them, was less than friendly with your wife and Mrs Cranworth at the times in question killed them both? Don't forget that the same unusual method—a garrotte—was used in each case. Doesn't it occur to you that there's almost certainly some connection between the two murders? Can't you understand the police are interested in this connection, whatever it may be?'

'Yes,' said Brooke-Brown weakly, and began to nod. He looked dreadful, and Tansey didn't need Sergeant Sester's whispered warning that the man couldn't take much more.

'Well, just one last point, Mr Brooke-Brown,' Tansey said. 'Then perhaps your doctor will give you a sedative, and you can have a sleep.'

'You mean you're not going to arrest me?'

'No, of course not. Just tell us where you were on—' Tansey referred to Sester for the exact date. 'On the night Jean Cranworth was killed.'

Many people would pause before remembering where

they were on a specific date two weeks ago, but not Donald
Brooke-Brown. Without hesitation he said, 'I was at home
all the evening. We both were, Catherine and I. We watched
a video of *Casablanca*, and read and talked and went to bed
early.'

'You have a good memory,' said Tansey without a hint
of sarcasm, though Brooke-Brown's statement contradicted
what Gainsford had told them he had overheard.

'Not really,' said Brooke-Brown without false modesty,
'but there is something I have remembered that could be
important.'

'Oh yes?' Tansey wondered what was to come.

'There was a phone call that night. It was after the ten
o'clock news. When I answered, whoever it was mumbled
something and put down the receiver. It could have been a
wrong number, but it was a woman's voice, and somehow
I got the impression it was Jean Cranworth. Of course I
could be wrong.'

'Why should she phone you?'

'Not me. Catherine.'

'But she didn't ask to speak to your wife?'

'No. She didn't.' Brooke-Brown was clearly regretting
that he had ever mentioned the phone call.

'Perhaps she thought her husband Harry might be there,
but when you answered she assumed he wouldn't be.'

'I don't know what you mean.'

'Don't you, Mr Brooke-Brown?'

There was a silence. Then Brooke-Brown brought his fist
down on the table with a great thump. 'For God's sake stop
asking me all these questions,' he cried, and his voice rose
hysterically. 'I didn't kill Catherine! I didn't kill Jean! I
haven't got the guts.'

And he began to cry, with great choking sobs like those
of a small boy.

CHAPTER 11

'Damn it all, they're nothing but a mob of bloody liars,' said Chief Inspector Tansey savagely. 'You can't trust one word any of them utters.'

'No, sir,' Sergeant Sester agreed, suppressing a grin.

'What's more, they don't seem to give a damn if you catch them out. They just say "Oh, sorry," and think of another lie to keep you quiet for a few days.'

'You've got the Cranworth brothers in mind, sir?'

'Among others, yes. I wouldn't trust the Gainsfords, either. He certainly didn't tell us all he knew, and in retrospect I can see that she was extremely defensive.'

Tansey was thoroughly exasperated, and sighed heavily. It had been an annoying morning in every sense. The investigation, beyond noting the obvious similarity between the attacks on Jean Cranworth and Catherine Brooke-Brown, had been able to add little of significance. No one in the mews had admitted to seeing or hearing anything untoward the previous evening. If a delivery man had called at the Brooke-Browns' house with what might have been a box of flowers, no one had heard Catherine speak to him or noticed him at all. No one had even noticed Donald Brooke-Browne's performance in the street after his discovery of his wife's body. Tansey's only comment was, 'They must all sleep like the dead in that damned mews.'

Donald Brooke-Brown, having at last been put under sedation, was sleeping off his shock in the Gainsfords' guest room. The routine search of the Brooke-Browns' house had, however, revealed the details of his Lodge and preliminary inquiries by other officers had already established that Mr

Brooke-Brown had attended the meeting the previous night, but had left when it ended, saying he felt slightly unwell. This was satisfactory as far as it went, but it was frustrating that no attempt to interrogate Brooke-Brown further about his movements after he had left the meeting would be possible until he had recovered.

Even more frustrating had been Tansey's interview with Harry and Steve Cranworth. As soon as they had been able to leave the scene of Catherine Brooke-Brown's death the Chief Inspector and Sergeant Sester had hurried to Manchester Square. It was still early in the morning, and Tansey had hoped to catch the Cranworths before they had heard of this second tragedy, so similar to their own. He had, however, reckoned without the radio and breakfast-time television.

'Come in! Come in!' said Steve. 'We were half-expecting you, Chief Inspector, though perhaps not quite so soon.'

The two brothers were not yet dressed, but were still in pyjamas with towelling robes over them. But they had showered and shaved and they exuded an aura of masculine freshness that made both Tansey and Sester feel grubby and dishevelled. There was also a tantalizing smell of coffee and bacon and eggs coming from Steve's kitchenette which reminded the officers that they hadn't eaten since the previous evening.

'You've come about Catherine,' said Harry at once. 'We've just heard the news on the radio and TV. First Jean, and now Catherine. It looks as if you've got a weirdo to deal with, and a dangerous one at that.'

Clearly the news had travelled fast. The thought flashed through Tansey's mind that a police officer might have made himself a few extra quid by tipping off a chum in the media, but even on his home ground he wouldn't have voiced such a suspicion. And, anyway, the damage was done. Whatever shock Harry and Steve Cranworth might have felt originally, they had got themselves well under control by the time the police officers arrived.

Tansey choked back his disappointment and responded to Harry. 'You may be right, Mr Cranworth,' he said. 'Or else that's what the killer would like us to think. Your wife and then your mistress. Do you think someone could hate you enough to destroy all the women close to you?'

'I sincerely hope not.' Harry sounded appalled.

'From that reply I gather that Catherine Brooke-Brown *was* your mistress, Mr Cranworth?'

'If by that old-fashioned term you mean that we were lovers, the answer is yes.'

'And you, sir?' Tansey turned to Steve Cranworth. 'Had you shared the lady's favours? Were you and she lovers too?'

'Briefly. But ages ago, and before my brother. She preferred Harry, and I lost interest.' Steve gave a sardonic smile. 'Poor Donald, what a life he must have led! Still, as they say, one shouldn't speak ill of the dead.'

'Neither of you seem to be unduly upset at Mrs Brooke-Brown's death?' Tansey remarked casually.

'Of course we're upset,' said Harry, glancing at his brother. 'I am especially, perhaps because I've got more reason than Steve. But somehow there's no awful feeling of horror, as there was with Jean. I can't explain why, but I'm sure you know what I mean.'

It was clearly an honest answer, and Tansey accepted it. He said bluntly, 'You know perfectly well what I have to ask. Where were you both last night?'

'Here,' the Cranworths replied in chorus, and Steve added cynically, 'As you can imagine, we're not being exactly overwhelmed with invitations at the moment. Though every single one of our pals is sure we're wholly innocent, they're all just waiting—to make certain, shall we say?'

'You can't blame them,' Harry said.

Tansey paused and then returned to his main theme. 'So

neither of you left this flat the whole evening?' he repeated.

'That's right. From the time we got back from our respective places of business we've both been right here till now.'

So they had alibis which were unverifiable, and therefore useless, Tansey reflected bitterly. Out of the corner of his eye he saw Sester's Adam's apple moving up and down as he swallowed in sympathy with his superior's unexpressed thought. Or perhaps he was swallowing because the smells from the kitchenette were becoming unbearable. Clearly, Tansey thought, both he and his sergeant were in need of their breakfasts. Besides, they would learn no more from the Cranworths at present. Once they had lost the chance of surprise there had been little hope.

But as they were entering the lift, it was left to Harry to spring the surprise. 'Chief Inspector,' he said suddenly, 'I told you that I wouldn't name the lady I was with the night that Jean was killed. I'd promised her I wouldn't. She didn't want to be involved in a murder and have her name splashed across the papers. At the time I intended to keep that promise, come what may. But circumstances have changed —dramatically, you might say. It was Catherine Brooke-Brown I was with, at her cottage near Richmond. I expect you can check on that.'

They had checked on it as rapidly as possible. Mrs Brooke-Brown's cottage was fairly isolated, but there had been lights in the windows that evening, and her car had been seen in the drive. Of course, none of this proved that Harry Cranworth had been there with her, but it did refute Donald Brooke-Brown's statement that she had been at home. What was more, it jibed with what Paul Gainsford said he had overheard.

'A lot of bloody liars,' Tansey repeated sadly. 'If only there was one of them—just one—that you could believe.'

*

The next morning, after her husband had gone to Seymour Street and his day's work, Hilary Tansey was shopping in the Marylebone High Street. She had gone into the newsagent's to buy a copy of the *Economist*, which she knew Dick liked to study, when she noticed her surname in the headline of one of the tabloids, with an old photograph of her husband beneath it. She glanced along the shelf and saw that most of the rest of the popular press had similar leads and pictures.

Hilary picked up one of the papers and glanced at the story. It said that this was the officer in charge of one of the nastiest murder cases in London's West End in years. And who was he? Not one of the best officers from the murder squad, but an officer on exchange from a rural force, with little experience of city crime. The public interest, the paper thundered, deserved better than this.

At this point she heard an acid voice challenge her. 'If you want to read that paper, you'd better pay for it. This isn't a public library.'

Scarlet with embarrassment, Hilary fumbled in her purse for the money and hurried away, forgetting the magazine she had intended to buy. She was angry with herself for not having flung down the rag and stormed out of the place. She was resentful at the assistant's sarcastic manner. But most of all she was indignant that anyone should write and publish such hurtful, lying rubbish about her husband.

By the time she reached the flat, she had her feelings under control, and had even reached the point of admitting that the assistant had had a certain amount of justice on his side. She let herself into the building, and because the shopping-bag was heavy, decided not to follow her usual practice of getting exercise by walking up the stairs. She therefore surprised Mrs Horner and Mrs Meade who, deep in conversation, had not been expecting her sudden emergence from the lift.

There was a moment's silence, which left Hilary in no doubt that she and Dick—and almost certainly the morning papers—had been the subject of their discussion. Then Mrs Meade quickly remarked that she must get on with her work and, with a brief nod to Hilary, stumped upstairs. For her part, Mrs Horner was not so easily disconcerted.

'My dear, I've got the kettle on for some coffee,' she said. 'I always believe the best way to make coffee is the simplest —just pour very hot water over the grounds and let it stand. So you must come and share it with me. It'll be ready in five minutes.'

'I'm sorry—' Hilary began, when the flood of words eased momentarily.

'No, no. You can't refuse me again.' Mrs Horner was not to be gainsaid. 'You've promised me so often, dear, but you always find some excuse not to accept an invitation. I'm beginning to feel you don't like me. Surely you can spare an old lady a little of your time.'

Hilary thought of a raft of excuses, but she knew when she was beaten. Besides, Mrs Horner was quite right. She had promised, and she could spare the time. What was more, in reality she quite liked Mrs Horner. But, she told herself, she was not going to discuss Dick and, whatever Mrs Horner might hope, she would do her best to avoid any but the most trivial comments on the murders.

'All right,' she said, almost too effusively. 'I'm sorry. It's very good of you. Thank you very much. I'd love to come, just as soon as I've put my shopping away.'

Once she was alone, Hilary's first impulse was to call Dick. But wiser counsels prevailed; she had made it a practice to trouble him as little as possible when he was at work, and she realized that by now he must also have seen the press stories, and there was no way she could help him.

Five minutes later Hilary was knocking at the Horners' door, which Mrs Horner had left ajar for her. When she went in, she was surprised by the appearance of the flat. It was much larger and more spacious than the one the Tanseys were occupying. It was also beautifully furnished, with some fine antique pieces. Naturally, as Hilary had expected, everything was spick and span and shone with polish, not unlike Mrs Horner herself.

'What a lovely place you have,' Hilary said, following Mrs Horner into the sitting-room, where a coffee tray was already laid.

'I try to keep it nice.' There was pride in Mrs Horner's voice. 'But David, being a man, isn't as tidy as he might be.'

She couldn't prevent herself gesticulating proudly towards what was obviously an extremely good professional studio portrait of her son, and she left Hilary to look at it while she went to fetch the coffee. As Hilary had expected, it had been taken by a very well-known photographer, and she was impressed. But she was more interested in the photographs that stood next door to it. One, clearly taken some years ago, was of a man in the uniform of an army officer, whom she guessed was the late Mr Horner. The other was of a girl, attractive without being pretty, and bearing a certain likeness both to David and to Mrs Horner.

'That's a very fine photo of David,' Hilary said as Mrs Horner returned.

'It was a present to me from him. He's very fond of his mother.' Mrs Horner made no effort to hide her satisfaction.

'But naturally. Why shouldn't he be?' replied Hilary, hoping that she didn't need to stay too long, making this kind of meaningless conversation. In the meantime, to play her part and for something to say rather than out of real interest, she asked, 'And the girl? She's not your daughter, is she?'

'Oh no. David's an only child. That's June, David's fiancée. She's his second cousin, too, on my side of the family, which accounts for the slight resemblance I expect

you've noticed—and you couldn't find a more suitable or
pleasant girl. I keep telling him she won't wait for ever. I'm
not a possessive mother, you know. I've always encouraged
him to go out with girls.'

Mrs Horner sighed gustily as she poured the coffee and
passed a cup to Hilary. 'Between you and me, dear, he says
he finds June dull, and he wants someone exciting and
vibrant, as he puts it. Exciting and vibrant, I ask you!
That's not the sort of girl who wants marriage and a normal
life, and my David's getting on. He ought to settle down.'

'I expect he can't face up to the idea of marriage and the
changes it would bring,' said Hilary, thinking of the pass
David Horner was said to have made at Natalie Smythe,
and wondering if being an actress made Natalie exciting and
vibrant in David's eyes. 'Anyway, you make him perfectly
comfortable here so why should he give up such a pleasant
way of life?'

Mrs Horner shook her head slowly. 'I don't know,' she
said, 'but he was all set to marry June about a year ago and
then . . . It's my private opinion that he met someone else,
though he wouldn't admit it. I've got an idea it's some local
girl. Ah well, let me pour you another cup, my dear, and
we'll talk about something else, like your husband and these
dreadful murders.'

From Hilary's point of view, this topic, though perhaps
less boring than David's love-life, was also less desirable. To
her surprise, however, Mrs Horner was courteous enough
to make no reference to the unsympathetic stories in the
morning papers, and fortunately she was prepared to do
most of the talking, so that few contributions were required
from her guest. Surreptitiously Hilary looked at her watch.
Ten more minutes, she thought, and she would retreat.

The doorbell halved that time. '—as I was telling Natalie
Smythe, she must never open her door except on the chain,
not with all this going on.' Mrs Horner continued to speak

as she went to answer the bell, and Hilary seized her chance.

She followed Mrs Horner into the hall and, when the old lady had brought in the box of laundry that had just been delivered, thanked her, and said that she really must go. Slightly to her surprise, Mrs Horner made no effort to detain her.

Instead she said, 'And you take the advice I gave Natalie Smythe too, my dear. Never open your front door except on the chain, especially if you're alone in the evening when your good man's out on duty.'

'No. No. I won't,' Hilary said, but she was startled. Somehow she had never thought of herself as particularly vulnerable, but presumably neither had Jean or Catherine Brooke-Brown. Only Pamela Greyling—or rather her husband—seemed to have considered that any danger might be personal.

Chief Inspector Tansey had, of course, seen the newspapers as soon as he reached his office. He thought about them for a moment, and then shrugged. If the Yard wanted to react, so be it. Otherwise, until further orders, he would do his best to prove the media wrong. But it rankled that he should be termed a 'rural' officer.

He rang for Sergeant Sester, who glanced at the tabloids on his superior's desk. 'If you'll permit me to say so, sir,' the sergeant ventured, 'I shouldn't take much notice of that nonsense.'

'I won't,' said Tansey shortly. 'Let's get down to it. The Cranworths defeat me for the moment, but Brooke-Brown should be capable of answering a few straight questions today. We'll concentrate on him.'

To the relief of the Gainsfords, a relief which Alysia made no attempt to hide, Donald Brooke-Brown had returned home. He had asked the Gainsfords to telephone his mother, and she had driven up from Kent the previous afternoon

and taken charge of the situation. As soon as it was permit-
ted, she had expressed her gratitude to Paul and Alysia for
their neighbourly help, removed her son to his own house,
and ensconced him in the guest room. She herself had spent
the night on the sofa in the sitting-room. She would have
had no hesitation in using the main bedroom, but its door
had been left sealed by the police.

Mrs Brooke-Brown, Senior, opened the door when Sester
rang the bell, but she kept the chain firmly in its place. A
formidable lady in her early seventies, she regarded the two
officers coldly

'If you're reporters you can go away at once,' she said
firmly. 'We have nothing to say to you.'

'Police,' said Tansey. 'Detective Chief Inspector Tansey
and Detective-Sergeant Sester.'

Mrs Brooke-Brown was accepting no one's word. 'So.
Well, prove your identities for me. Please,' she added as an
afterthought.

'In the circumstances, it's best to be cautious,' she commented, after she had carefully inspected their warrant
cards and let them into the hall.

They found Donald reclining on the sofa in the sitting-
room in his pyjamas and dressing-gown. He glowered at
them and scarcely returned their greetings, but his appearance was considerably improved. He could, Tansey thought
cynically, plead shock no longer.

Brooke-Brown may have lost this excuse, but he had
acquired a new shield, in the shape of his mother. As Tansey
commenced his interrogation, it became clear that Mrs
Brooke-Brown intended to intervene constantly.

'Let's start with the Lodge meeting,' said the Chief Inspector, omitting to mention that Brooke-Brown's presence
there had already been confirmed.

'Your Cousin Gordon will remember you at the Masons,
Donald,' Mrs Brooke-Brown prompted immediately.

'I don't think he was there, Mother,' Brooke-Brown protested, but he went on to identify several fellow-members who would certainly vouch for his presence and the time of his departure at the conclusion of the meeting.

Tansey then began to press him about his later activities —his precise itinerary, anyone who might recall seeing him or speaking to him, on the streets or in the pub he claimed to have visited.

'You must remember something,' Tansey insisted when Brooke-Brown hesitated. 'Come on,' he said, 'you're wasting our time. It's vital for all of us that you cooperate.'

Tansey spoke with authority, and Donald Brooke-Brown, contradicting himself several times, slowly and reluctantly produced a few street names. The Chief Inspector decided to change his line of questioning.

'Mr Brooke-Brown, you must admit your behaviour last night was odd,' he said at length. 'Can you explain it? Had you quarrelled with your wife again?'

'Again? What do you mean, again? Catherine and I don't quarrel.'

Tansey ignored the sulky response which he knew to be yet another lie. 'Or had you just discovered that, however much she denied it, your wife was with Harry Cranworth during the night Jean Cranworth was killed?'

'She was not! She was here with me!'

'Mr Brooke-Brown, Harry Cranworth swears she was with him, at her cottage near Richmond.'

'He's a liar, a dirty, filthy liar! He's saying that out of spite because—because she gave him up. I asked her to, and she agreed. She promised me.'

'Look, Mr Brooke-Brown, we know you had already had one row with your wife about Harry Cranworth. And you don't really believe she kept her promise, do you? She was *not* here with you the night Jean Cranworth died. You know that—and we know it too. What's more, you suspected where she really was that night.'

'No! No! No!' Forgetting his role of semi-invalid, Brooke-Brown rolled off the sofa on to his feet. He stood, glowering at the two officers, and he was suddenly a surprisingly menacing figure. 'How dare Harry? How dare he? I— I'll—'

They were never to know what threat Donald Brooke-Brown was about to utter, though his intention was clear. Mrs Brooke-Brown had risen also. She looked ludicrously like her son.

'Chief Inspector, I protest at what in the circumstances is a most brutal police interrogation. Catherine was not the most faithful of wives—I never approved of the marriage— but Donald was devoted to her. He's just recovering from the most appalling shock, finding her as he did. You can't expect him to concentrate on your irrelevant questions about—'

'Madam, my questions are not irrelevant,' Tansey broke in icily. 'I am investigating two extremely unpleasant murders. If you'd prefer that I take your son to the Police Station, I shall be happy to do so.'

There was a moment of silence, broken by Brooke-Brown, who put his hand over his mouth and ran. A door banged. A bolt was shot home. Donald Brooke-Brown had taken temporary refuge in the lavatory.

Mrs Brooke-Brown turned on Tansey. 'You've made the poor boy ill, Chief Inspector,' she said accusingly.

Tansey didn't apologize. He nodded to Sester and said, 'We'll be going, Mrs Brooke-Brown. Please tell your son that his movements on the night of his wife's death will be checked rigorously, and you might add—'

'He didn't do it. My Donald would never—'

Tansey ignored her. 'You might add that we'll be back, Mrs Brooke-Brown. Good day to you.'

*

'Poor old dear,' said Sester unexpectedly as he got into the car beside Tansey. 'She's scared for her beloved boy, I suppose.'

'She may have cause,' said Tansey.

'You think that, sir? From what we've learnt about Catherine Brooke-Brown I can understand Donald wanting to get rid of her. She sounds as if she were a real bitch. But what did he have against Jean Cranworth?'

'Nothing personally, I imagine, but Jean was Harry's wife and Donald's a fairly screwed-up character. He hates Harry, and between them Harry and Catherine may have driven him just that bit too far. Having decided to kill Catherine, he could have resolved to kill Harry's wife first, as a form of revenge.'

'It's a neat theory, sir.'

'Too neat,' said Tansey. 'I don't believe a word of it. I don't really think Donald Brooke-Brown is capable of a double murder. And nor do you.'

CHAPTER 12

Late that Thursday afternoon, as Alysia Gainsford sat curled up on the sofa watching television, the glass of sherry and the plate of small macaroons that she allowed herself at this time of day on a table beside her, her doorbell rang peremptorily. Reluctantly, she got up, and looked out of the window to see who it was. When she sighted Mrs Brooke-Brown, Donald's mother, in the mews below she sighed; one way and another she had had enough of the Brooke-Browns to last some time. But she was a kind woman and, as the doorbell pealed again, she went downstairs.

'I'm sorry to bother you,' said Mrs Brooke-Brown as the door was opened, 'but have you seen Donald?'

'Donald? No.' Alysia choked back a desire to laugh. The question might have concerned a lost child or even a cat, rather than a grown man. Then something of Mrs Brooke-Brown's anxiety communicated itself to her and she said, 'Come in and tell me what's happened.'

Mrs Brooke-Brown came into the little hall. She told Alysia that she had decided to have a rest, and had gone fast asleep. When she woke, Donald was no longer in the house. He had left no message, but just disappeared.

'He's probably gone for a walk,' said Alysia Gainsford, anxious to reassure her neighbour, 'or to the shops to buy something.'

'He almost never goes for walks,' said Mrs Brooke-Brown, 'and what would he want to buy? No, it's not that. Somehow I'm—I'm afraid.'

Alysia stared at the older woman. 'Afraid?' she queried. She hesitated before asking the obvious question, then decided to be blunt. 'You mean he might try to—to do something stupid, to do away with himself?'

'Yes. Yes. But—but afterwards—'

'After what?' Alysia was normally a placid person, not fond of drama; in her opinion there had been too much of that recently in their ordered lives—thanks to the Brooke-Browns. 'After what?' she repeated in exasperated tones.

'After he'd—he'd killed Harry Cranworth,' said Mrs Brooke-Brown. 'He hates Harry Cranworth, though he really shouldn't blame the man.'

She hesitated, as if considering whether to say more, then went on, 'Unfortunately Catherine was one of those women men find irresistible, though heaven knows why. I'm sure you agree. She wasn't beautiful. She had a child's body, and her head was too big for it. But she—she exuded sex, and she was prepared to set her cap at any man who took her fancy, married or not.'

By this time Alysia Gainsford had recovered from her momentary bewilderment at this sudden outburst. 'Quite,' she said calmly. 'I certainly don't disagree with what you say. But Catherine's hardly a problem now, is she, Mrs Brooke-Brown? Assuming your guesses about Donald are right, the problem seems to be what, if anything, to do about Harry Cranworth.'

'And about Donald himself,' his mother said quickly.

It occurred to Alysia that saving a potential victim was of more immediate importance than protecting his possible killer. She said, 'I think the best idea is for you to come upstairs with me and have a glass of sherry to steady your nerves. You can watch by the window in case Donald returns, and I'll do my best to telephone that policeman Tansey.'

Mrs Brooke-Brown was far from sure that this was a good idea, but the aggression she had felt towards Tansey earlier in the day when he was questioning Donald had evaporated in her fear for her son's physical safety if he attacked Harry Cranworth—and his legal position if he succeeded in killing the man. By this time Mrs Brooke-Brown was feeling old and drained, and it was a relief to let Mrs Gainsford take control. She followed Alysia upstairs without argument.

Although she was a mild woman who liked to let her husband make important decisions for the family, Alysia Gainsford could, when necessary, act forcefully and with determination. This was such an occasion. She would have much preferred to have been left alone until Paul returned from his office, but as the Brooke-Brown family and its affairs had once again encroached on her privacy she would cope with the situation. She wished, she told the operator in no uncertain terms, to speak to Detective Chief Inspector Tansey. The matter, she added without being asked, was urgent, and was related to the murder of Mrs Catherine Brooke-Brown. It took some persistence, but she refused to be fobbed off on anyone else, and eventually she was put through to Tansey.

Tansey had spent a busy afternoon, in the course of which it had been agreed that the Yard's Press Office should issue a statement, outlining Tansey's career and emphasizing that, far from being an officer from a so-called 'rural' force, his experience of criminal investigation in large cities was considerable, and certainly comparable with that of any officer of similar rank in the Met. It would conclude by expressing the Met's complete confidence in Detective Chief Inspector Tansey, and in his ability to bring this investigation to a successful conclusion.

The Chief Inspector was relaxing for a moment, when his phone rang yet again, this time with Alysia Gainsford on the line. Tansey thought it prudent to be polite but distant. When she began to retail her story his interest rose, and he listened carefully and thanked Alysia for her information. After a moment's reflection he was about to say that he was sorry, but he could not, on the basis of the little that seemed to be known, authorize an immediate police search for Donald Brooke-Brown, when Sergeant Sester, after the briefest of knocks, burst into the office.

'Sir!'

Some odd instinct made Tansey say, 'Hang on a moment, Mrs Gainsford.'

Then he put his hand over the receiver and said to Sester, 'Don't tell me that Brooke-Brown has shot Harry Cranworth, confessed to the murder of those two women, and drowned himself in the lake in Regent's Park?'

Sester stared at the Chief Inspector in awe. 'You must have been reading the cards, sir, though it wasn't exactly like that.'

'What wasn't?' In spite of his momentary instinct, Tansey hadn't been taking Mrs Brooke-Brown's forebodings, as relayed by Alysia Gainsford, with any great seriousness, considering them the worries of an old woman about her precious son.

He gestured to Sester to keep quiet for a moment, and he said, 'I'll phone you back, Mrs Gainsford. You're at home, I assume. Stay there.' He put down the receiver. 'Now, Sergeant, what *has* happened?' he demanded.

'Well, there seems to have been some confusion, but as far as I can gather it was like this, sir—'

Half an hour later, in a bare interview room at the Maryle-bone Police Station in Seymour Street Donald Brooke-Brown glared at Tansey as if defying the Chief Inspector to contradict him. Brooke-Brown looked in a bad way. One side of his face was swollen and distorted, and he obviously had had a nose-bleed, but the police doctor who had examined him had said that he was not seriously hurt. Harry Cranworth, on the other hand, was in hospital, while his brother, Steve, was in another room in the Station awaiting Tansey's attentions.

Brooke-Brown was fully prepared to make a confession, and anxious that Sergeant Sester should take it down accurately. In fact, he was so eager that Tansey found it hard to stem the flood while he cautioned the man. Certainly, Brooke-Brown waived any wish to see a solicitor.

Yes, he said as soon as he was allowed to speak, he had attacked Harry Cranworth and caused him bodily harm—or whatever it was called nowadays; his intent had been to kill the bastard. Only his own inefficiency and circumstances over which he had no control had prevented him from succeeding. He was only sorry he hadn't managed the job.

'I waited for him outside his house,' Brooke-Brown said. 'I'd planned the whole thing carefully. He's bigger than me, and stronger. I wouldn't have had a chance in a straight fight. Look what Steve did to me.' He pointed at his face. 'Anyway, as I say, I *wanted* to kill Harry. I thought that if I could only take him by surprise I could push him under a car or a truck. The traffic moves fast round the Square and with luck—'

But at the crucial moment Donald Brooke-Brown hadn't been blessed with what he would have called luck. Granted, he had been successful in taking Harry Cranworth by surprise outside the Manchester Square house. He had butted him in the stomach, and sent him stumbling into the road almost under the wheels of a large blue Mercedes.

It was true that Harry could easily have been killed, but two things saved him. First, Brooke-Brown had been a trifle over-eager, so that Harry fell further in front of the Mercedes than had been intended, and secondly the driver's reactions were superb. He braked hard and flung the heavy car away from the falling body that had so suddenly appeared. He was not able to miss Harry completely but, as subsequent X-rays were to prove, Harry suffered only slight concussion, some bruises and a couple of cracked ribs.

Steve had been with his brother at the time and his first concern—shared by the driver of the Mercedes—was to ensure that Harry was not badly hurt. Someone in the offices on the lower floors of the Cranworths' house telephoned for the police and an ambulance. Then the driver went to inspect his Mercedes which, in its attempt to avoid Harry, had damaged a parked car. The road was blocked. There was a great deal of hooting and confusion as cars tried to back away from the scene, until the authorities, under the first impression that this was a mere traffic accident, appeared to sort out the chaos.

Throughout all this Donald Brooke-Brown sat on the pavement by the Cranworths' front door, hugging his knees which he had pulled up to his chest, as if for warmth, and rocking to and fro like some Korean peasant. From time to

time he shivered violently. Someone, thinking he had been
hurt by the car, put a rug round his shoulders and would
have helped him to the ambulance when it arrived.

But Steve Cranworth was having none of this. Seeing
Brooke-Brown being led away, he was at once reminded of
the true sequence of events and what the wretched man had
tried to do to Harry. He launched himself towards Donald,
pushed aside his escort and punched Brooke-Brown in the
face. It was some seconds before the police were able to pull
him away.

'And they're accusing *me* of assault,' he said indignantly
to Tansey, when at last his turn came to be interviewed.
'*Me*. I ought to be at the hospital with poor old Harry.
Instead, here I am, being treated like a criminal.'

'You shouldn't have tried to take the law—' Tansey
started to say weightily.

'—into my own hands. Nonsense! Bugger that for a lark!
What about that bastard Brooke-Brown?'

After a while Steve calmed down and, after being cautioned, gave his version of events, which Sergeant Sester
duly took down.

'OK,' said Tansey when Steve Cranworth had finished.
'I'll see what we can do for you.'

'But I'm not going to hurry about it,' he added to Sester,
when Steve had been hustled away by a constable.

'I don't blame you, sir,' said Sester.

'Still,' said Tansey, 'it's obvious we've got to charge them
both. Brooke-Brown can so readily deny his confession
of attempted murder, or at least claim that he was so
overwrought as to be unfit to make a statement, that I think
we'll go for something less to start with—grievous bodily
harm, say. We'll keep him overnight, at least. In the circumstances the beak'll probably refer the case to a higher court
and set a reasonable figure for bail. Any simple public order
offence will do for Steve Cranworth, and we'll let him

go tonight on his own recognizance. I'll check with the Prosecution Service, and you try to arrange for the cases to be heard in the Magistrates' Court tomorrow, if possible.'

'Yes, sir,' said Sergeant Sester, knowing it would be late before either of them got home that night.

CHAPTER 13

The Marylebone Magistrates' Court was packed the next morning. Tansey and Sester were there, of course, together with a number of witnesses to the fracas in Manchester Square the previous day. The presence of friends and relations of the defendants wasn't surprising, and nor was the strong media representation. The public, too, seemed to have learnt that the cases were coming up, and had turned out in force, presumably because this was an opportunity to see some of the people closely involved in two appalling murders.

The night before, Dick Tansey had been so late in getting back to the flat that he had had little opportunity to discuss the case in detail with Hilary, as was his usual practice. Their conversation on the subject had been limited to recriminations about the stupidity of the tabloid press, and satisfaction with the Yard's statement, which had been widely reported in the evening papers and on radio and television. Tomorrow evening, Tansey promised, they would go into the case in detail; by then the hearing in the Magistrates' Court would be over. At first Hilary had wanted to be present in court but, in view of the possible embarrassment that might arise because representatives of the media were likely to be there in force, Tansey had advised against it. In the end, Hilary had seen his point and acquiesced.

Donald Brooke-Brown was put up in the dock first, a pathetic, miserable figure, with his face still bruised and swollen; a night in the cells had done nothing to improve his appearance or his morale. He stared straight in front of him, and ignored his mother who, nobly accompanied by Alysia Gainsford, was trying to send him encouraging signals across the court. Whether he was beyond caring what happened to him, or was playing a part his lawyer had prescribed for him, Tansey couldn't decide.

The prosecution stated their case, called their witnesses, and suggested that further charges might follow. The magistrate nodded understandingly, and Tansey thought that all was going well.

It was now the turn of the defence. '—mind unbalanced with grief at the death of his wife, whom he adored,' the lawyer was intoning. 'He comes on the man who, rightly or wrongly, he believes to have been her lover, and attacks him. Of course the attack was not premeditated. Sir, that alleged confession the prosecution introduced was made under strain, if not wholly invented. If the police themselves believed it, why is the charge not more serious—attempted murder, say, or at least attempted unlawful killing—'

'Sir,' the solicitor for the prosecution intervened, 'I hope you will bear in mind that the police did suggest that other charges might be forthcoming.'

'So what does that mean, sir?' continued Brooke-Brown's lawyer. 'That the police aren't sure, and need time to make up their minds? That is not the way justice is done in this country. No, Mr Brooke-Brown's act was reprehensible, no doubt, but it was the act of a sad, sick man. And did he attempt to escape afterwards? No. He waited for the police, only to be assaulted by the man's brother. You can see for yourself—'

But the magistrate had had enough. 'Mr—er,' he said. 'I appreciate what you say, but you are not addressing a jury at the Old Bailey. The case is adjourned for two weeks, so that we can see if further charges are to be preferred. If so, the matter may well be resolved in a higher court. In the meantime, in view of your submissions, I will release your client on bail of a thousand pounds, and on the strict condition that he keeps well away from Mr Harry Cranworth.'

'A sensible decision, sir?' Sester murmured to Tansey, while the deflated defence lawyer thanked the magistrate and set off to assist with arranging bail.

'Very sensible,' commented Tansey.

Brooke-Brown was led from the court, and there was a certain amount of shuffling and whispering as those present relaxed. Old Mrs Brooke-Brown and Mrs Gainsford left immediately, presumably to collect Donald. Journalists, one or two of whom Tansey had already come to know by sight, hurried out to phone in their stories. Some members of the public had lost interest and were ready to follow them. But among those who stayed Tansey recognized his neighbour, Mrs Horner, who was talking animatedly to her son, David, and pointing in his direction. Tansey swore under his breath and turned to Sester.

'Here comes Steve Cranworth, sir,' said the sergeant.

Steve Cranworth had decided not to be represented by a solicitor, and to plead guilty to a charge of common assault. He had already been heard as a witness in the previous case, and he retold his story simply and with conviction. When he had seen Brooke-Brown sitting on the pavement, his anger had erupted and he had attacked him. He agreed that he shouldn't have done so, but at the time and even in retrospect he felt he had had some justification—and he hoped that the magistrate would agree.

The magistrate did agree. Steve Cranworth was fined a hundred pounds, and bound over to keep the peace for a year. The outcome of both cases had been predictable, but

Tansey was disappointed that the time in court had brought no fresh insight into either of the deaths he was investigating.

In spite of the best efforts of the uniformed constables on duty and the court authorities, there was no way that Tansey and Sester could avoid the reporters in the corridor immediately outside the courtroom. To Tansey it seemed that the area was full of men and women—many of whom were clutching microphones, and most of whom were firing questions at him simultaneously. At least, Tansey had time to reflect, cameras were forbidden inside the building. But outside . . .

Those questions he could hear in the general mêlée seemed to him either impossible to answer, or directed towards establishing his own inefficiency. The influence of the Yard's supportive statement had been limited and had worn off quickly, at least as far as the popular press was concerned.

'Any hope whatever of arresting the killer yet?'

'Making *any* headway at all, Chief Inspector?'

'Why do you find London so difficult, Chief Inspector? Different from your own patch, eh?'

'How long have you been a Chief Inspector?'

To all such queries Tansey could only reply, 'No comment at this stage. A press conference will be held when it's appropriate.' With an expressionless gaze he pushed his way ahead, thankful for Sester's presence beside him, and he couldn't have been more grateful when Sester suddenly seized him by the elbow and directed him down a side passage and through a door marked 'Private'.

Sester bolted this door behind them. 'This way, sir. It's all arranged, though we didn't expect such a mob,' he said. 'But that's done the vultures,' he added with satisfaction. 'If you follow me, there's a back exit that will bring us out among the dustbins, and I've made sure our car's parked close by. Then we'll be off before any of that lot's twigged what we're doing. They're not very bright, really.'

Tansey laughed. 'Well done, Sergeant,' he said. 'I don't know what I'd do without you.'

Sester grinned his pleasure at the remark. 'So now we go and visit the sick, you said, sir,' he remarked. 'No need to take flowers or fruit, is there?'

'None.' Tansey was firm. 'Between you and me, Sergeant, I thought Harry Cranworth got no more than he deserved —if only for obstructing the police. He's been a damned nuisance to us.'

'I couldn't agree more, sir, but I doubt if he'll see it that way.'

Sester, however, was proved wrong. At the private hospital to which Harry Cranworth had been transferred as soon as it was established that his injuries were minor, he had a large room with an en suite bathroom to himself. There was a police constable sitting outside the door, but he was present more to keep away the press than because Harry was believed to need protection. Indeed, the officer's main task seemed to be receiving the flowers and gifts that were arriving in a steady stream for the invalid. Thanks to the media, the news of Harry's misfortune had spread fast, and it was clear that he had many well-wishers.

'Now you behave yourself, Mr Cranworth!' Tansey and Sester heard the nurse say as they knocked and immediately entered the room.

The girl, who was young and pretty, had obviously been rearranging Harry's pillows when he had caught her around the waist. She looked as though she were embracing him, though in fact she was struggling to free herself. Seeing the two officers, Harry laughed and let her go. She regained her balance and, red-cheeked, vented her annoyance on the new arrivals.

'Who are you?' she demanded. 'If you're journalists—'

'Police,' said Harry Cranworth regally. 'I'll vouch for them. Off you go, my girl. You've made me very comfortable.'

But as soon as the young nurse had left his demeanour changed. He waved Tansey and Sester to chairs and, before they could speak, surprised them by asking about Donald Brooke-Brown. He sounded anxious, and it was evident that he was serious.

'Mr Brooke-Brown's out on bail,' said Tansey noncommittally. 'But he shouldn't bother you again.'

'I know what happened in court, Chief Inspector. Steve phoned to tell me. But what's going to happen to him? What's all this about further charges? Certainly I'm not going to prefer any. I wouldn't have let the police arrest him in the first place if I'd had anything to do with it,' he said earnestly.

'I'm afraid the question of charges and proceedings is out of your hands now, Mr Cranworth. Mr Brooke-Brown will be prosecuted,' said Tansey. 'After all, he did deliberately try to push you under a car, didn't he?'

'Oh, sure, but he had some provocation.' When Tansey and Sester involuntarily exchanged glances but didn't contradict him, he said, 'Personally, when he comes up again I shall volunteer to be a witness for the defence. What's more, if you put me up for the prosecution, I'll have no alternative but to appear as a hostile witness. Steve should never have hit him, though mind you I hope I'd have done the same thing in Steve's place.'

Sester stared at his shoes, which needed a good polish, and Tansey stared at Harry Cranworth. Neither of them was able to accept this suddenly reformed and remorseful Harry. After all, they had just caught him making a pass, casual though it may have been, at an attractive nurse.

As if reading their thoughts, Harry continued, 'It's OK. I've not been struck by a flash of light from heaven, and it's

not the result of my concussion. I've no regrets for screwing
Brooke-Brown's wife. If it hadn't been me it would have
been someone else—and often was, I might say. But after
Catherine had been garrotted just like—like poor Jean—I
shouldn't have lied as I did.'

'And which of your lies are you talking about now, Mr
Cranworth?' Tansey asked resignedly.

Harry grinned. 'I asked for that one,' he admitted. 'Listen.
Originally I told you—and it still holds true—that I
wouldn't name the friend I was with the night Jean was
killed. Then I said it was Catherine. She was dead. She
couldn't deny it. I hoped it would get you off my back, Chief
Inspector, and stop all this nonsense about obstructing the
police, and so on. I didn't realize it would send poor old
Donald round the bend.'

'So that was a lie, too?'

'Yes. Frankly, I've no idea where Catherine was that
night, or who she was with. Maybe her latest boyfriend,
whoever he may be. But she certainly wasn't with me.'
Harry spoke with conviction. 'Will you tell Donald that you
know that for a fact, Chief Inspector? It won't stop him
hating me, I'm well aware. For some reason he's always
resented me more than her other men. But it might make
him feel a little better about Catherine.'

'People are quite extraordinary,' said Dick Tansey.

It was nine o'clock that evening. In slacks and slippers
and a shabby old pullover, the Detective Chief Inspector
was off duty, lying sprawled in an armchair in what was at
present his living-room. The lights were on. The curtains
were drawn. Rain gusted against the windows, and there
was an occasional rumble of thunder. After a pleasant day
London was having a storm. But inside the flat it was warm
and cosy.

With Hilary in a long housecoat, sitting opposite him and busy knitting, the Tanseys might have been any ordinary couple. Their only claim to peculiarity was the serious nature of the discussion they had been engaged upon concerning the Marylebone murders, as the media insisted on calling them. One evening paper had even gone so far as to suggest that with these events taking place so close to Baker Street, the Yard should find a medium who could call upon the shade of Sherlock Holmes to assist the provincial Chief Inspector. Tansey was pleased to note that he had been promoted from 'rural' to 'provincial'. In any case, failing a consultation with Holmes, he found that a discussion with Hilary helped to clarify his thinking, and he valued his wife's judgements and opinions.

'Then you believe Harry Cranworth this time?' she asked at length.

'On this point about Catherine Brooke-Brown, yes. He's got absolutely no reason to lie about it. On the contrary, in fact. Because all he's done is get me on his back again in an effort to make him support the alibi he says he's got. But he still refuses to give me his girlfriend's name, though I've promised to be tactful and keep her husband out of it. He says he's given his word. He's an odd mixture. As I said, people are odd.'

For a minute or two they were silent, though their thoughts were running on similar lines. There was no doubt that pressure on Tansey to find the villain was increasing daily, though in fact he was no nearer to bringing the case to a conclusion. And the press criticism still rankled with them both.

Hilary, who was not the most experienced of knitters, dropped a stitch and swore softly. Tansey smiled sympathetically. He could appreciate her frustration. She didn't take naturally to domesticity, and would have much preferred to be beside him in Sergeant Sester's place. But even if they hadn't come to London the baby would have made that impossible, and they both wanted the baby.

To change the subject slightly, he said, 'Guess who was in court this morning. Our dear neighbour, Mrs Horner, with a terribly smart hat and her son, David. I thought he worked.'

'He does. He's got quite a responsible job in the travel agency in the Marylebone High Street.'

'He wasn't there today.'

'No. Apparently he did another chap's duty last week, and this day off was repayment, as it were.'

Tansey laughed aloud. 'Now how on earth did you get to know that, darling? Have you been having another fireside chat with Mrs Horner?'

Hilary shook her head. 'No. This time it was with David himself. I'd gone to the Public Library, and I met him there. He said he often spends his free days in the Reference Room, reading up about foreign parts. He claimed that it makes his work more interesting, which one can understand.' She smiled broadly. 'He also said it was sometimes difficult to concentrate at home because his mother liked to talk so much.'

They shared the joke, and Tansey said, 'He seems to have done an awful lot of talking in the Reference Department. I thought they had signs saying "Silence" all over the place. Didn't anyone object?'

'Good heavens, Dick, with that carrot-haired Gemma Fielding sitting there at her desk we wouldn't have risked more than one whisper in the Reference Room. You should have seen the disgusted look she gave poor David when he dropped a book.'

'I can imagine it. After all, I've met the lady.'

'No, David and I walked back from the library together,' Hilary explained. 'He told me he'd been in court this morning because his mother hadn't wanted to go alone. But

I think he was quite curious himself. I tried to ward him off talking of the murders by asking about his fiancée, but she clearly isn't his favourite topic at the moment. So we settled for the library and his work. Luckily it's not a long walk, so I survived.'

'You seem to have had a surfeit of the Horners lately.' Tansey sighed. 'I hope you're not being too bored here, darling.'

'Of course I'm not. Stop worrying about me, Dick.' Hilary folded up her knitting, put it in its bag and stood up. 'I'm going to make us some tea. Then I suggest bed.'

Tansey smothered a yawn. 'Two excellent ideas,' he said. 'Tomorrow may be a Saturday, but it's a working day for me. There's a conference at the Yard in the morning, and the case is sure to be mentioned.'

CHAPTER 14

Yes, reflected Tansey as he set off the next morning, it's perfectly true. A policeman's work is never done—especially when he's in the middle of a major inquiry. Weekends, for example, were usually a good time to find witnesses at home, and a few hours could often be snatched for busy officers to hold conferences. And even if villains did take weekends off—which they didn't—Saturday and Sunday sometimes represented a couple of days in which there was some chance of catching up with bulging in-trays.

He spent the morning at the Yard and the afternoon at his desk, and by five o'clock he leant back, feeling that he had done a good day's work. His self-congratulation was interrupted by the phone, and he gave a silent prayer that some fresh horror was not about to be reported. He was both

uneasy and annoyed when the caller announced himself as
Paul Gainsford.

But Gainsford reassured him. 'This is a social call, Chief
Inspector—or almost. I was wondering if you'd come
and have a drink with me, when you're off duty, as it
were.'

The slickness of the approach and the charm of the voice
didn't deceive Tansey. Gainsford was nervous, and he had
something he wanted to get off his chest to the police. It
might or might not be important, but it couldn't be ignored.
Still, the Chief Inspector hesitated; it was hardly in accordance with the book for the officer in charge of a murder case
to join a suspect—however remote—for a so-called social
drink. Nevertheless, he decided, rules were made to be
broken.

'Now—this evening, do you mean?' he asked, trying not
to sound reluctant, but relinquishing his hope of getting
home early.

'Splendid! See you in half an hour or so, then?' Gainsford
was clearly relieved and delighted; having made up his
mind to say whatever he had to say, he didn't want to be
frustrated. 'Can you come down to my club—it's the Oxford
& Cambridge in Pall Mall. I'll meet you in the hall.'

Tansey's knowledge of London's clubland was slight,
mainly gleaned from books and magazine articles, but his
taxi-driver naturally knew the building, and the Chief Inspector was thankful to find Gainsford waiting in the club's
imposing hall. The neat little man was leaning against a
counter chatting easily to a porter. He came forward at once
to greet his guest.

'Bang on time. Well done,' he said, as if they were old
friends. He nodded towards a big book on a stand on the
porter's counter. 'I've already signed you in, so come along
and let's see if we can get a drink.'

Tansey followed him up wide marble stairs. He caught a

glimpse of a large high-ceilinged dining-room before Gainsford led him into an equally splendid smoking-room, furnished in typical club fashion with deep, comfortable leather
armchairs and sofas and small tables. The area of the room
was about double that of the whole of Tansey's Marylebone
flat, but the Chief Inspector was determined not to be
overawed.

The room was empty, and Gainsford said, 'This place is
rather like a morgue over the weekend, even though it's one
of the few remaining clubs that provides meals and service
on Saturdays and Sundays. But at least we'll be nice and
private.'

He waved Tansey to a chair and went to ring a bell. A
waiter appeared with surprising speed, and drinks were
ordered. While they waited for them Gainsford delivered
a monologue about the club, and how useful it was for
entertaining clients. It was quite evident that the impression
Tansey had received over the phone had been right, and
that Paul Gainsford was nervous.

'. . . Today, for instance,' he said, 'a couple for whom
I'm doing over an old mill were just passing through London, and I was able to give them lunch without all the
hassle of a restaurant. We had a good long chat before they
went off to Heathrow.'

Tansey had no choice but to listen to this nonsense, but
when the drinks came, he glanced deliberately at his watch
to show a certain impatience. Gainsford noted the rebuke,
but he still seemed loath to come to the meat of the matter.
Instead he sipped his vodka and tonic reflectively.

At last he said, 'Chief Inspector, I'm not very proud of
what I have to tell you—' and he stopped.

'Mr Gainsford—'

'Oh, Paul, please—'

'Mr Gainsford,' Tansey repeated firmly. Socializing with
suspects had its limits, and he was glad to find that

Gainsford took the hint and made no attempt to address him other than formally for the rest of the evening. 'Mr Gainsford, I'm not interested in your pride—or your morals, if they're involved. If you know something that might help to find the murderer of Jean Cranworth and Catherine Brooke-Brown it's your duty to tell me. Withholding information from the police about a serious crime is a serious offence. You know that as well as I do. However—' Tansey relented slightly— 'unless it's essential for the conduct of the inquiry, whatever you've got to say will be kept strictly to our police personnel.'

Gainsford looked far from convinced, but he nodded, took a couple of large gulps of his vodka, and said, 'All right. To begin with, I have to admit to being an inquisitive individual.' He paused.

'So?' said Tansey.

'I mean I'm fascinated by people and their foibles. Maybe I should have been a psychiatrist rather than an architect —even though in my business one comes across some oddballs.' He paused again. 'Donald Brooke-Brown is an oddball. No normal man would have put up with Catherine. He let her treat him like a—a doormat. I can't think of a more original simile, or one that's more appropriate. His wife was constantly unfaithful to him, and she taunted him with her—her adventures, but nevertheless he continued to worship her.'

There was yet another pause, and Tansey decided to take the initiative. 'You were one of her—er—' he started.

'Her victims? Yes, I suppose I was. She didn't care a damn about me, but my wife went away for a few days to look after her sister who'd had an operation, and Catherine decided to add me to her collection. I must have been mad to risk my happy, stable marriage, but—but, well, I'm sure you've learnt enough about Catherine to understand. Luckily she didn't find me very—very satisfactory, shall we say?—and when Alysia came back she dropped me.

Needless to say Alysia doesn't know, though I'm afraid she may suspect.'

'I understand,' said Tansey, and thought that Paul Gainsford had just provided himself with two potential reasons for wishing Catherine dead. First, on his own admission she had cast him aside, as a romantic novelist would probably put it; he might not have accepted this rejection as readily as he had suggested. Secondly, it would apparently not have been out of character for her to threaten to tell his wife. On the other hand, there seemed no conceivable reason why Gainsford should have wanted to kill Jean Cranworth.

Tansey said, 'You spoke of Catherine's "victims", Mr Gainsford. I can't see Harry Cranworth as a "victim", can you?'

'No. Indeed he wasn't,' Gainsford said at once. 'He took Catherine—literally—on his own terms, and enjoyed her. They had what you might call a special relationship. That's why Donald focused his hatred on Harry.'

'And how do you know all this? Why are you so sure?'

Gainsford returned to his hesitant manner, obviously embarrassed by what he had to say. He had not objected to admitting to his brief affaire with Catherine, though naturally he wanted to keep it from his wife. So this was different, Tansey thought. This was something of which he was truly ashamed.

Gainsford finished his vodka and tonic at a gulp and went to ring the bell. When the waiter came he ordered the same again. Tansey made to protest, but the malt whisky he had been drinking had been extraordinarily smooth, and anyway Gainsford was paying no attention to him.

His second drink seemed to buttress Gainsford. He said, 'I told you I was an inquisitive man. In fact, I've got to admit I'm a little worse than that. I'm a sort of intellectual Peeping Tom, I suppose. Or do I flatter myself? Oh,

certainly I don't creep around looking through lighted
windows at girls in their underclothes. I just simply get a
kick from finding out what makes people tick. That sounds
almost poetic, doesn't it?'

Gainsford gave a nervous, forced laugh, then went on.
'When I get a chance I eavesdrop on people's conversations.
I'm afraid I'm not sure I'd be above opening someone else's
letter if it were delivered to my place by mistake, and it
looked interesting. And I ask leading questions—tactfully,
of course—use *Who's Who*, and all the other sources. You'd
be amazed, Chief Inspector, how much I know about my
neighbours.'

Tansey did his best to hide his surprise. Gainsford's
normally pale cheeks were scarlet and there were beads of
sweat on his upper lip. He buried his face in his glass and
drank. Tansey felt sorry for the man, and decided to try a
little psychology himself.

'As long as you don't actually interfere with the mail or
annoy anyone, there's nothing wrong in all this, is there?
Curiosity's a widespread human trait. Certainly you could
argue that my job's almost entirely concerned with it. There
are many worse—er—social sins, surely?'

Gainsford stared at him. 'You mean—you're not
shocked?' he demanded.

'Shocked, no. Not in the least. Mildly surprised, perhaps,
but that's all. Don't be silly, Mr Gainsford, or else you'll be
needing a psychiatrist yourself one of these days. Now,' the
Chief Inspector went on briskly, 'you mentioned neighbours. Of course the Brooke-Browns are your closest neighbours—and they seem to make a habit of airing their
differences in public.'

Tansey's treatment had restored some of Gainsford's
self-confidence. 'Not exactly in public,' he replied. 'But they
often have their windows open, and upstairs there's a thin
wall. I—I listen deliberately. In spite of what you just said,

I'm not proud of it, but I do.' He stared at Tansey. 'I can rely on you to—er—to—'

'To keep the details of your—your eccentricity to myself? Yes, indeed, Mr Gainsford. It's what you know that's of primary importance to the police. How you learnt it is only of interest if it helps us to judge whether we can rely on you and your information. I gather this is all hearsay evidence, anyway.'

'My God, this conversation has relieved my mind!' Gainsford rubbed his hands together. 'It calls for another drink.'

He was across the room and ringing the bell before the Chief Inspector could stop him, even if he had wished to do so. In fact, drinks served in London clubs are normally larger than those sold in pubs or bars, and the two malts were doing their work. Tansey was beginning to enjoy this rather odd episode.

He waited until the drinks had arrived, then said, 'Mr Gainsford, I can't help feeling all you've said has been a kind of preamble. I'm sure there's something really important you want to tell me. What is it?'

'Yes.' Gainsford, himself now suitably relaxed, responded at once. 'You remember the occasion when I was washing my car out in the mews? I told you about it, but not everything. What I didn't tell you was that I heard Donald threaten Catherine—really threaten her. He said, "I warn you, Catherine. You've gone too far. You're going to end up like poor Jean Cranworth—and you'll deserve it!" Oh, and he called her a bitch, for good measure. I'm not sure I've given you his exact words, but they're pretty close. I've a first-class memory, and at the time what he said kind of jolted me. I thought that at last the poor worm had turned.'

'And you'd be prepared to swear to this in court?' Tansey asked.

'If it were essential, yes,' said Gainsford. 'I'd say I have excellent hearing and the Brooke-Browns' windows were open. All true. I wouldn't have to say I crept as close as I could to listen, would I? But you remarked that anything of this kind would be merely hearsay evidence.'

'It would, literally,' said Tansey. 'But I suspect that in the circumstances a judge would admit a report of such a definite threat.' He wondered if Gainsford could be believed, and if a case could be built against Donald Brooke-Brown on this foundation. Then he said, 'Mr Gainsford, thank you very much for your information—and for the excellent whiskies.'

'My pleasure.' Paul Gainsford, having accomplished what he had considered to be his duty, was showing signs that he too was ready to leave. 'Do you have a car?' he asked, and when Tansey shook his head said, 'Then we'll get a cab. Perhaps I could drop you off wherever you want to go.'

And twenty minutes later the taxi stopped outside Tansey's block of flats. The Chief Inspector was feeling unusually cheerful, probably because of the three malt whiskies. He had no means of knowing that, even as he ran up the stairs to his flat, the killer of Jean Cranworth and Catherine Brooke-Brown was planning his third murder.

The murderer had not originally planned to act again so soon, but he had learnt that the police were methodically inspecting all lock-up garages, and he was afraid that the stolen motorbike would be found. He thought of leaving it in a public parking place where, if it were noticed, it couldn't incriminate him. But then it wouldn't be so readily accessible, and retrieving it would present danger. Besides, some thief might steal it, and he would have to acquire another; the irony of this possibility made him grin.

There were other problems, too. His box of flowers had received harsh treatment and was looking battered. It needed to be replaced. Even the flowers themselves were

beginning to disintegrate and smell. The police statement
had warned that entry to the homes of the Cranworths and
the Brooke-Browns might have been gained by someone posing as a delivery man, but flowers had not been
mentioned specifically. He considered alternatives, but
only the prospect of flowers seemed guaranteed to work on
women.

Nevertheless, he decided not to return to the same florists,
though they had been obliging and had made no comment
on his slightly unusual request for the blooms to be packed
in a box to deliver oneself; plastic shrouds were more usual.
Come to think of it, the flowers themselves were not essential,
but it would be even more unusual to ask for a florists' box
without any flowers. And the police might know more than
they had admitted.

That, of course, was a constant fear, but this third effort
was special, because the victim was a very special lady. It
had to succeed. As he thought of tightening the garrotte
around her neck he smiled with satisfaction. If all went well,
it would be a significant job satisfactorily accomplished—
if all went well.

CHAPTER 15

To Chief Inspector Tansey a week without developments
seemed a very long time. He suspected that to his superiors
it seemed even longer. But there was little or nothing he
could do about the unfortunate situation. Certain routine
inquiries continued, but in the main Tansey found himself
at his desk in Seymour Street amid piles of paperwork with
occasional opportunities for morose contemplation of the
state of play. He was glad when Friday came again, with
its prospect of one or even two rest days—days on which

he hoped he might forget the Marylebone murders, days he could devote to Hilary.

It was seven o'clock on that Friday evening when Steve Cranworth returned from his office to his Manchester Square flat. He was not in the most equable of tempers. It had been a typically bad day for a publisher. One of his bestselling authors who rarely came to London had turned up without warning, and had expected red-carpet treatment in spite of the lack of notice. He had been forced to cancel an important appointment and postpone a long-scheduled meeting. And the damned woman hadn't even been grateful; she had done little except complain about the lack of advertising for her books.

Steve flung his briefcase on to the sofa. It was heavy, for it contained a bulky manuscript he knew he should find time to read before Monday. It wasn't really vital, but he prided himself on keeping up with his work, whatever or whoever else might occupy him or interfere with his plans or his routine. He was thinking about the weekend ahead —and about Gemma Fielding—when the phone rang.

'Harry?'

Steve recognized the soft breathless voice at once, and made a point of not answering it by name. 'No. It's Steve. Harry's gone back to live in his own place. You've got the number, haven't you? Call him there.'

'No, I can't. There's no time. Give him a message, Steve. Please. Tell him I'll be free tonight. Nine o'clock.'

Steve hesitated, then he said resignedly, 'OK, I'll try, but I may not be able to get hold of him.'

He sighed with exasperation. The line had already gone dead. He tapped out his brother's number, but there was no answer. He would have to try again later. He decided to have a drink and a light supper; after an expense account lunch with his author he was the reverse of hungry. He opened a bottle of Riesling and made himself a mushroom omelette. Afterwards he washed up the few utensils he had used, and tried Harry's number again. He shrugged when there was still no reply.

At about half past eight Steve Cranworth left the building. It was a dark night, for the moon was new and the cloud-cover low, but it wasn't cold. Steve, who had spent the day at his desk or in an over-heated restaurant, felt that he needed some exercise, but it was a long walk to Hampstead and he decided to take his car, as usual.

The block of so-called 'mansion' flats in which Gemma Fielding lived was typical of the many such buildings scattered about London. Built about the turn of the century, from the outside they appeared to be large and ugly red-brick piles. But in many cases their façades belied their pleasant and spacious interiors.

Gemma's flat consisted of one large room, a smaller bedroom and a bathroom and kitchenette. She had brought a sixty-year lease with a large mortgage when she moved to London and took up her position at the Marylebone Public Library, and had never regretted her decision. By now the flat was nearly as she wished it to be, and anyone who judged the flamboyant carrot-haired woman by her external appearance alone would have been amazed at the fine furniture and *objets d'art* that Gemma had so carefully and tastefully collected.

Steve stood on the outer steps, rang the bell of Gemma's flat, and waited for her voice to come over the entry-phone. Although their affaire had lasted some while she had resolutely refused to give him a key. He smiled at the familiar crackle before he heard her say sharply, 'Yes. Who is it?'

'It's me—Steve. Honey, I want to talk to you.'

'But I've no intention of talking to you. Go away! Now!'

'Gemma, Gemma, love, I've said I'm sorry. What more do you want?'

'Go away! And don't call me "love". I'm not your "love"! Not any more! If you don't stop bothering me I shall call the police.'

The handset upstairs was banged down, the connection abruptly cut. 'You bitch! You'll be sorry,' Steve said aloud and involuntarily.

Simultaneously he was aware of the door in front of him opening to let a man and a woman emerge. He saw his chance. 'Good evening,' he said cheerfully, and began to move into the hall as if by right, only to find his way barred by a man in slacks and a T-shirt, taller and considerably broader than himself.

'And just where d'you think you're going, mister?' the man demanded fiercely.

'Actually, to visit Miss Fielding—if it's any of your business,' Steve retorted.

'It certainly is my business, because I'm the caretaker here, see. I look after the block—and I look after the tenants too. What's more, I was in the hall when you were talking to Miss Fielding on the intercom. You can hear every word. It's not made for private conversations. So you get going, Mister Steve whoever, and don't come nosing round here again unless she invites you. OK?'

Steve Cranworth opened his mouth to protest, but found that a large hand had splayed itself across his chest and was pushing at him. Caught off balance, he staggered backwards, and fell, landing half in the gutter where he caught the side of his face on the bumper of his car that he had managed to park outside. Cursing, he got to his feet, but by then the front door of the block of mansion flats was firmly shut. There was nothing more he could do at the moment.

'Are you sure you'll be all right, darling?' Hector Greyling asked anxiously for the umpteenth time. 'It's too bad of the PM to demand my presence at Chequers at such short notice. I've got the briefing papers for the meeting on Monday morning, and I can't imagine why it needs to be brought forward like this. Nor can I imagine why it should go on so long that I've got to stay the night. And if we're staying, wives might have been invited too.'

'Never mind, darling. Presumably it's all for an important reason,' said his wife, wishing that he'd go. 'Anyway, the food will be good there—probably better than at the Stanboroughs'.'

Greyling grunted. 'Nevertheless, I'd much rather be dining with the Stanboroughs as we'd planned,' he said. 'And it's unfortunate this should happen the first time they've invited us.'

'Surely they'll understand that you can't refuse the Prime Minister.' A trace of irritation had crept into Pamela Greyling's voice.

She sat at her dressing-table and regarded her beautiful face as she slowly removed her diamond earrings. She had never asked herself what might have happened to her if she'd been born plain. She knew. She only had to remember her elder sister, Dorothy, whose so-called 'love-match' had come unstuck after eighteen months, leaving her with no support, but pregnant with a first child. Dorothy's answer to that problem had been the gas oven. Pamela had decided that whatever happened there was no way she would follow her sister's example. There was one easy way to avoid that possibility—marrying money. And, with her face and figure, that hadn't proved too difficult.

'Perhaps you should have gone alone,' said Hector Greyling, still ruminating about their cancelled dinner date.

'Oh no, Hector. Lady Stanborough was obviously frightfully relieved when I said I wouldn't be coming either. She pressed me, of course, but only out of politeness. I'd have completely upset her table. And in fact I have got a headache, so perhaps it's all for the best.'

She swivelled round as her husband came up behind her, and returned his kiss warmly. She was fond of Hector, who was kind and generous and in most ways considerate. That he was also possessive and intensely jealous was a price she had to pay.

'Take care,' she said. 'And don't let that new driver go too fast.'

'I won't,' he promised, happy that she should be anxious about his welfare. 'I suggest that you have supper as soon as I've gone and then go to bed, darling,' he added. 'Take a little aspirin for that headache.'

'I will,' she said.

There was champagne cooling in the refrigerator, smoked salmon, cold pheasant and fresh fruit salad, all left-overs from a boring ladies' luncheon party she had been forced to give. Now she was glad of the remains, which would make an excellent meal. If only Harry had got her message . . .

Alysia and Paul Gainsford had also been invited out to dinner that Friday. They had considered the traffic, and left their house at seven-thirty so as to arrive at their friends' Kensington flat at eight. Alysia enjoyed the evening, but she noticed that Paul seemed rather quiet. She was disappointed but not surprised when comparatively early he signalled that they should leave. When they reached home, she was about to suggest bed, when Paul said that what he needed was air and that he wanted to go for a walk. It was eleven o'clock when Paul set off and, according to both himself and his wife, he returned before midnight.

Old Mrs Brooke-Brown had spent almost all her time since seven that evening waiting anxiously and watching the mews from the sitting-room window. She had cause to be worried, for Donald had seemingly disappeared yet again.

Until tonight, apart from attending Catherine's funeral, he hadn't left the house since his appearance in court a week ago. Instead, he had apparently succumbed to despair, becoming increasingly apathetic and indifferent, hardly bothering to exchange a sentence with her. But at about six-thirty she had suddenly discovered that he was no longer anywhere in the house. Apparently he had simply walked out without any warning.

As the hours passed and her anxiety grew she considered phoning the police, but she was afraid that Donald might have broken the condition of his bail and gone after Harry Cranworth again. She could think of no other action to take and, in between making herself cups of tea—she had no desire to eat—she sat by the window, waiting. She almost wished Donald was safe in a prison cell; then she wouldn't need to suffer this unending anguish.

Shortly before one in the morning, Mrs Brooke-Brown, who by now was half-asleep in her chair, sat up abruptly. There were sounds in the mews below, an engine running, the slamming of a car door, and now angry voices, one of them Donald's. She stood and looked out of the window, fully awake.

There was a taxi directly beneath her. Donald was leaning against it as if not strong enough to stand upright. The driver was preparing to get out of his cab and he was shaking his fist. It wasn't difficult for Mrs Brooke-Brown to interpret the scene; Donald had taken a taxi home, but didn't have enough money to pay the fare. Seizing her handbag, she hurried downstairs.

'What's the trouble?' she demanded.

'I'm waiting to be paid what I'm owed,' the driver said aggressively. 'If not . . .' He gestured towards his radio.

'All right, all right,' said Mrs Brooke-Brown at once. 'You'll be paid. Donald, how much—' But, ignoring his mother, Donald Brooke-Brown had gone straight into the house. She turned and addressed the driver. 'How much is the fare?'

'Twenty pounds.'

'Twenty pounds? Where have you come from?' Mrs Brooke-Brown had plenty of courage. She walked around the vehicle and inspected the meter. 'Don't be silly,' she said. 'You could lose your licence for overcharging like this.'

'I'm not overcharging, lady.' Confronted by a seemingly reasonable woman, the driver had lost some of his aggression. 'What's on the meter is the fare from Leicester Square, but I've got to go home now and clean my cab. I'll have to fumigate it before I can get another fare. There's vomit all over the rear seat. Look and see if you like.'

He switched on the light in the back of the taxi and Mrs Brooke-Brown took one quick glance. The man was right. Donald—She felt she wanted to cry. She found two ten-pound notes in her handbag. She wasn't going to argue further with the driver.

'Here you are,' she said. 'And I'm sorry about the cab.'

'OK, lady. Thanks.'

Biting back her tears, Mrs Brooke-Brown went inside the house and locked the front door. At least Donald was home, she thought. She need worry no longer about where he might be. In fact, he was sitting half way up the stairs, his face buried in his hands. His suit was torn and dirty—and he smelt of vomit and filth. More importantly, there was blood oozing from a cut among his hair. All Mrs Brooke-Brown's motherly instincts came to the fore.

'Oh Donald, my poor boy!' she said, tears reappearing in her eyes. She knelt in front of him.

Slowly he raised his head, and she gaped. The damage that Steve Cranworth had inflicted on him had disappeared, except for some slight remaining discolouration of the skin. But now he had new injuries, and worse ones. His cheeks were lacerated and bleeding, as if they had been deliberately raked by someone with long nails. One of his front teeth was missing and one eye was closed.

'Dear God!' said Mrs Brooke-Brown. 'Where have you been? What's happened? We must get a doctor.'

'No. No. No doctor. The police might get to hear of—'

'Yes,' said Mrs Brooke-Brown. 'I see. Well, where have you been?'

'Out,' Donald said. 'I went out. I couldn't stand it here any more in this house. Catherine's house. And knowing that by now she's just ashes—grey ashes . . .'

'Darling, she wanted to be cremated,' Mrs Brooke-Brown said gently. 'She stipulated it in her will.'

'I don't care! It's horrible to think of. Ghastly!' The words whistled through the gap in his teeth.

Mrs Brooke-Brown sighed. She hadn't liked her daughter-in-law. She was prepared to admit to herself that she hadn't grieved over her death—only the manner of it. But the effect on Donald had been traumatic in the extreme. She wondered fleetingly when he would realize that, thanks to Catherine, he would be a rich man when the will was probated.

'All the same, Donald,' she said. 'There's no excuse for going out and getting disgustingly drunk.'

'I didn't. I'm not drunk,' he protested, and certainly he showed none of the obvious signs of inebriation. 'I've had a couple of drinks. No more. And I went to the cinema.'

'Then how on earth did you get in this state?'

'I was mugged. I didn't like the film and when I came out there were two men and a girl. They pushed me down an alley and they took everything. My wallet. My watch. Even my signet ring. And—and they misused me. I can't tell you. It was revolting. The girl tried to make me kiss her, and when I wouldn't she tore at my face. In the end they rolled me into a doorway and left me.'

'I see. But where was all this? The taxi-driver said Leicester Square. Were you in Soho, of all places?'

'Yes.'

Mrs Brooke-Brown regarded her son doubtfully. She didn't know whether to believe him or not. 'Well, there's only one answer, Donald. Bath and bed. Come along now.' She spoke as if he were ten years old.

The third victim was dead. Gemma Fielding lay half in the narrow hall, half in her bedroom. She was fully dressed in long shocking pink velvet pants and a black silk blouse. Her feet were bare. Around her neck, digging into the flesh, was the inevitable garrotte, but there was blood on the carpet and even a smear on one of the walls, and some was seeping out from beneath Gemma's body—altogether a surprising amount of blood.

CHAPTER 16

'All right if we turn her over now, sir?'

'Yes. Turn her over, and get all the photography done, especially a close-up of the entry wound. Then I'll have another look at her.'

The pathologist got to his feet and watched as the two police officers carefully turned Gemma Fielding's body on to its back. The younger drew in his breath and half shut his eyes. It was not a pretty sight. Gemma's blouse had been ripped from top to bottom and the flimsy bra broken, exposing the perfect white breasts. Over her heart, where the bullet had entered, was a round dark hole, and there was dried blood everywhere over the chest and torso.

The pathologist frowned. 'Chief Inspector Tansey should see this,' he said.

Someone called for Tansey, who was in the bathroom, where there were obvious indications that the killer had made some effort to wash before leaving the flat. One officer was carefully wrapping a towel with signs of blood on it in a plastic bag, and an earnest young man in plain clothes was using tweezers to extract hairs from the washbasin. 'We'll have to have this trap off, damn it,' he was saying to his colleague.

Tansey edged his way along the narrow hall. The flat seemed full of people, too full for comfort. There was scarcely room to move, to do one's own job, without obstructing someone else. He gazed down at the unfortunate Gemma.

'Well,' he said, 'we know from the exit wound that she was shot, as well as garrotted—'

'And we've found the bullet, sir,' interrupted the scene of crime inspector. He was normally a dour man, but this success seemed to have elated him. 'It was in that wooden doorframe. We're doing the measurements now.'

He took a plastic envelope from one of his officers and held it out to Tansey. 'It looks like a .38 to me. Probably a Smith & Wesson, left over from World War Two perhaps.'

'You may well be right,' said Tansey. Then, to the pathologist, 'But which came first—the shooting or—'

'I'll let you know for sure after the PM,' said the pathologist. 'And I'm afraid that won't be till tomorrow morning.'

Tansey opened his mouth to expostulate, but the doctor went on quickly, 'I'm sorry—it's just plain pressure of work. But I'll tell you something to be going on with. She was quite unlike the other two lassies. She must have fought like a maniac. There's blood and tissue under her nails—that should help to cook the killer's goose, once you've found him. It looks as if we're going to be in the blood-typing business. Maybe we'll be able to try this new-fangled genetic fingerprinting.'

'Don't complicate matters,' Tansey replied. 'There's an awful lot of blood,' he added.

'I know,' said the pathologist. 'That's been bothering me. I can't account for it at the moment. It certainly didn't all come from those gunshot wounds, as you can perfectly well see for yourself. Anyway, I'll take all the necessary samples.'

'It looks as if she was killed near the front door, sir,' the scene of crime inspector intervened again, 'and dragged along here. Perhaps he intended to arrange her on the bed like the other girls, but either he was interrupted or he found her too heavy and abandoned the effort.'

'Or he got in a panic,' said Tansey. Then he added, 'Though he found time to wash, seemingly.'

It's a bit of a muddle, Tansey thought, but, please God, this time he's made mistakes and we're going to get him.

He turned back to the inspector and the pathologist. 'There's nothing more I can do here at present. I'm only in your way, and the way of the forensic chaps. So if anyone wants me I'll be downstairs in the basement flat talking to the caretaker and his wife. What's their name—Spenser, isn't it?'

'That's right, sir,' said the inspector. 'Luckily they seem a sensible couple. As soon as Mrs Spenser opened Miss Fielding's front door this morning—Saturday's one of her cleaning days—and saw the body, she went and called the police.'

Tansey nodded. 'So I gather. I'll look in before I leave,' he said, knowing from past experience that at this stage the scene of crime team would be happy to be without him. To the pathologist, he added, 'I don't need to say—'

'I know. I know. As soon as possible. I'll let your office know a definite time. Another weekend gone for a Burton,' said the doctor.

Tansey found Sergeant Sester chatting to the uniformed constable on duty outside the flat. Sester shook his head.

'No luck, sir. The people along the corridor are away on holiday, and the couple at No. 6 across there were at a dance last night and didn't get home till three. And no one else heard a thing, certainly not a shot. Anyway, a .38 doesn't make that much noise.'

'Too bad. Let's go and talk to these Spensers.'

Mr and Mrs Spenser were expecting them. They were shown into the kitchen, where the kettle was boiling. They were offered tea, and Tansey accepted gratefully for them both—his own late breakfast had been interrupted by the urgent call. The two officers sat down at the kitchen table with Spenser, whose bulk seemed to fill the space of two men. Meanwhile, Mrs Spenser, a small-bird-like woman in a flowered apron, made the tea and produced a plate of biscuits.

'Now, let's get this straight,' Tansey said affably when the tea had been poured. 'You're the caretaker here, Mr Spenser, and Mrs Spenser obliges, as they say, for some of the tenants. Is that right?'

Spenser nodded and his wife said, 'I went in to clean for Miss Fielding Wednesday and Saturday mornings. It's not a big flat, but she was very particular about her belongings.'

'And this morning?' Tansey encouraged her.

Mrs Spenser shuddered. 'I saw the blood on the carpet first thing, then her lying there. I recognized those pink trousers she wore at once. I shut the door real quick, I can tell you. I didn't take even a step inside the hall, and I came to tell Fred and he phoned your people.'

'Very sensible of you, Mrs Spenser,' said Tansey. 'I wish more witnesses would behave so correctly.'

Mrs Spenser flushed and looked doubtfully at her husband. When he nodded, she said, 'Chief Inspector, we think we know who did it—who killed poor Miss Fielding.'

'You do?'

'Yes, and we've got evidence,' Fred Spenser said.

'We think it was Mr Cranworth—Mr Steve Cranworth, the brother of the man whose wife was killed by that wire round her neck,' Mrs Spenser broke in. 'He and Miss Fielding were—were lovers. Had been for some months. But they quarrelled and she threw him out. He came round here once or twice, and I know he phoned her, but she wouldn't have none of him any more.'

'He was around here last night, threatening her.' Spenser spoke positively.

'What?'

This was the first item of really new information that the Spensers had produced. Tansey listened attentively as Fred Spenser recounted how he had come upon Steve Cranworth trying unsuccessfully to persuade Gemma Fielding to let him in the previous evening.

'They were talking over the entry-phone. She cut him off, but he was angry, and he went on arguing as if she could hear,' said Spenser. 'But it was only me who was listening. I was in the hall—I was just going off duty—and you can hear every word from there. I'll show you if you like, Chief Inspector.'

'Later, Mr Spenser. So what did Steve Cranworth say?'

'He said something like, "You'll regret this, Gemma. I'm warning you. I'll get you, my girl." Real threatening, he sounded. I soon sent him on his way.'

'You said, *something like* those words, Mr Spenser.'

Fred Spenser took a quick glance at Sergeant Sester, busy in a corner with his shorthand notebook, and he began to hedge. 'Well, I can't swear I've got it exactly right, Chief Inspector. But that was the general idea. Nasty and bully-ing, he was.'

Tansey nodded. He believed the story, though he sus-pected that Spenser had tended to exaggerate Steve Cran-worth's threats. 'Now, is there anything else you should tell me?' he asked. And when they both shook their heads, he thanked them for their help, the tea and the information.

'Upstairs before we leave, sir?' Sester reminded him.

'Yes.' Tansey had not forgotten. 'I promised we'd have another word with the inspector before we went.'

Once again the inspector seemed unusually cheerful, greeting them with a surprisingly wide smile. 'I think we've made another find that'll interest you, sir,' he said. He signalled to one of his officers, who brought over a plastic envelope in which was a pink oval-shaped object. 'A rose petal, quite fresh—and there are no roses in the flat,' he said proudly.

'Where was it found?'

'Actually, in the bathroom, sir. It could have adhered to the murderer's clothing, and dropped off when he went to wash. He might easily have failed to notice an odd petal, though he presumably collected the box and any loose flowers that might have been scattered around. Perhaps the box came open in the struggle the pathologist mentioned.'

'You're assuming that the victim opened the main door and then her own door to an unknown man because he says he's got flowers to deliver. Don't you think that's a bit odd in view of the murders, and the publicity they've received? I met her in life, and she seemed to me a sensible and determined woman.'

'I know, sir. I had the same feeling myself. But Hampstead's a good long way from the sites of the other crimes. A moment's forgetfulness, perhaps. And don't forget, as you pointed out yourself, women like flowers. I asked my wife, and she said she'd be too intrigued to send them away—as long as the man had some valid-sounding reason for delivering them late at night. She added that she'd know they weren't from me,' the inspector added somewhat dolefully.

'Well, maybe that's what happened,' said Tansey. 'After all, the caretaker or porter or whatever he is was off duty,

and she might not have wanted them left in the hall. I doubt
if we'll ever know for sure what happened. But it's true that
the rose petal might be a real lead. Try and get it identified
—all roses have names—and start inquiries right away, will
you, Sergeant—you know what's wanted.'

'Yes, indeed, sir. I'll get on the phone immediately. It's
going to be a busy weekend.'

With Sergeant Sester at his elbow Tansey pushed his way
through the throng of reporters and photographers that had
already gathered outside the block of flats. He no longer
cared how stupid they made him look, or what inaccurate
rubbish they wrote about him. He was determined to finish
this case—and was convinced, whatever the more flamboyant media might choose to think, that the man he was after
was no maniac, but a very cunning and devious villain.

'A devious villain,' Tansey murmured aloud.

'Yes, sir. Where to now, sir?' Sester said encouragingly,
fastening his seat-belt and starting the engine.

'Oh—Manchester Square.' Tansey seemed to wake from
a reverie, and realize that he was sitting in his unmarked
police car with Sergeant Sester at the wheel. 'With luck, as
it's Saturday, the Cranworths may be at home. You know,
Sergeant, I'm getting more and more convinced that they're
the key to these killings.'

'You mean one of them's guilty, sir?'

'No. I don't think that's necessarily so. But it can't be
coincidence that the three women were all closely connected
with the two brothers.'

Tansey lapsed into a silence which lasted until they
reached Manchester Square. Steve Cranworth was at home,
and let them in. He was up and dressed, but he had not
shaved, probably because of the lacerations on his face,
which in the morning light appeared ugly and purplish.

'Had an accident, Mr Cranworth?' Tansey asked.

'You could say that.' Steve Cranworth appeared to be tense and upset. 'Now, before you start asking me questions, will you tell me something? Why is it that whenever a young woman anywhere in London is killed you immediately come and see me?'

'Because the young women are always intimately connected with you and your brother,' Tansey said sharply.

'*Touché*.' Steve shrugged his shoulders. 'Poor Gemma! Why Gemma? It was like the others, wasn't it? All it said on the radio was that there had been another murder. Another young woman had been garrotted—and it gave her name. You may not believe me, but I'm shaken. I was fond of Gemma.'

'When did you last see her?'

'I went to see her yesterday evening, but I only got to speak to her through the entry-phone at the front door of her building. She won't—wouldn't—forgive me for claiming she'd been in bed with Harry and me together. But you know about that. Anyway, she wouldn't let me in.'

'And you just went away?'

'Not exactly.'

Steve Cranworth gave his version of the encounter with the caretaker. It differed very little from Spenser's. But Steve denied that he had threatened Gemma. He might, he agreed, have said she'd regret him, but he hadn't said that he'd 'get her'.

'It's not the kind of expression I'd use,' Steve said with distaste. 'Incidentally, did this chap Spenser tell you what he did to me? He put his great hand in the middle of my chest, and pushed—pushed hard. I wasn't expecting it, and I staggered across the pavement and fell half under my car. That's how my face got into this mess—on the underside of the bumper.'

'Really? Did you see a doctor?' Tansey's voice was quite dispassionate.

'Heavens, no. It's not that serious. It looks worse than it is. I came home, washed it and put some antiseptic on it.'

'Did you go out again later?'

'No. I'd hoped to spend the evening with Gemma. When that fell through, my face was so unbeautiful I had a drink or two and listened to music.' He smiled wryly. 'Again, no alibi, Chief Inspector.'

Tansey ignored the comment. 'So when did you actually *see* Miss Fielding last?'

'Thursday afternoon,' Steve answered promptly. 'I had some details to check for a book I'm editing, and I went to the Marylebone Public Library. As luck would have it, Gemma was on duty in the Reference Department, but she refused to talk. So I did my work, and then went to sit among the Faithfuls. I thought I'd wait till she went home, but—'

'What do you mean by "Faithfuls", Mr Cranworth?'

Steve sighed. 'That was what she called them. It's the same in all public libraries, I guess. There were a couple of old men who spent hours there for company, and warmth in winter. And an elderly lady who used to go to sleep over her book, and snore. And the chap who came to Gemma's rescue once when she had a slight accident with her motorbike in the Marylebone High Street; ever after he pestered her for a date, and eventually she had to be really unpleasant to him. And there's another chap who makes a point of asking her the most abstruse questions—'

'I see,' said Tansey. 'Regular readers, you might say.'

'Yes, except that most of them don't read much,' Steve agreed. 'Nor did I on Thursday. I kept on waiting for someone to come and take over from Gemma, but when it happened she was too quick for me and I missed her. She disappeared behind the scenes somewhere and I'd wasted my time.'

At this point they were interrupted by Harry Cranworth.

Still in pyjamas and a dressing-gown, his hair uncombed, he looked half-asleep. He regarded the officers balefully.

'Aren't you ever going to leave us in peace?' he demanded.

'Harry!' Steve began, but was interrupted by Tansey.

'Mr Cranworth,' the Chief Inspector said, 'there's been another murder, similar in method to that of your wife and Mrs Catherine Brooke-Brown.'

'What! Who? Someone we know?'

Harry was fully awake now. He flung himself into an armchair, but sat bolt upright. It was evident that, unless he was a very fine actor, he knew nothing of this third death.

'Who?' he repeated.

'Gemma,' Steve said.

'Gemma?' Harry shook his head in disbelief. 'Oh no.'

'Yes, Mr Cranworth,' Tansey intervened. 'Gemma Fielding was killed last night, garrotted. So, where were you last night?'

'Me?' Harry gave a mirthless laugh. 'I might have expected that. You suspect me, don't you, because Jean was my wife. But why should I want to kill the others?'

Tansey didn't answer him. He had noted that Harry's face, unlike his brother's, was unmarked and showed no sign of having been attacked by a terrified but determined Gemma.

'OK, I'll tell you where I was last night,' Harry continued angrily. 'I was with the same lady I was visiting the night Jean was murdered. I wouldn't give you her name then, and I won't now. You arrest me if you like, Chief Inspector, and try to prove I'm the guilty party. You'll have your work cut out.'

'I certainly intend to prove who it was that killed your wife and Mrs Brooke-Brown and Miss Fielding,' Tansey said mildly, getting to his feet. 'Whoever it may be, Mr Cranworth. And can you both tell me what your blood-groups are?'

If Tansey had hoped that the question would surprise or
worry them he was mistaken. Steve laughed. Then, reaching
for his wallet, he extracted a card which he offered to
Tansey.

'We're both the same. We always carry these in case we
have an accident in the street, or even at work—though
they're not so keen on blood transfusions as they used to
be, are they? We're both equally unusual, too, and both
much in demand to give blood. See—Group AB, Rh nega-
tive. There are less than two people in a hundred like us,
they tell me.'

'I see,' said Tansey. 'Thank you.'

'My card's downstairs,' said Harry, 'but it's an identical
story, as Steve said.'

'No need to bother,' said Tansey. 'Thank you both once
again for your help.'

CHAPTER 17

Detective Chief Inspector Tansey and Detective-Sergeant
Sester emerged from the house in Manchester Square to be
greeted by a succession of sharp barks. Tansey hardly had
to turn his head to realize that Wellington was being urged
along the pavement towards them by Mr Arbuthnot.

'Oh no!' said Sester, sighting the brown poodle and
remembering his last encounter with him.

Before Tansey could comment, Mr Arbuthnot had arrived at a trot, eager to greet them. 'I've been waiting for
you, Chief Inspector,' he said. 'I was in my sitting-room
and I saw you go into the Cranworths'. I must admit I was
on the look-out. After the dreadful news about the third
garrotting, I thought you might be coming here.'

'Good morning, Mr Arbuthnot,' said Tansey, smiling

encouragingly at the new arrival. He hadn't forgotten that this was the witness who had originally suggested that the killer might have gained access to his victim's home by pretending to deliver flowers—a possibility that the Chief Inspector hoped soon to confirm.

'Yes,' Tansey said, 'I'm afraid it's another similar affair —and similarly horrific.'

'And you've been questioning the Cranworth brothers again?' Mr Arbuthnot's eyes were bright with excitement. 'I would gamble that Harry Cranworth didn't tell you what time he came home last night, or rather this morning. Did he?'

Tansey couldn't give Arbuthnot a direct answer to this one. Instead, he said, 'I'm sure you're going to tell us, sir.'

'Yes. Yes, indeed I am—and more than that.' Mr Arbuthnot was triumphant. 'It was like this. We—that's Wellington and I—we were taking our usual morning outing. At about half past six, or a little after, a taxi comes roaring up to the Cranworths' house and out gets Harry. He pays the man and hurries indoors, but the taxi waits a minute—perhaps the cabby thought I might be another fare—and so I walked right past it.'

'One taxi's much like another,' said Tansey doubtfully.

'Of course!' Mr Arbuthnot stared at the Chief Inspector and somewhat acidly agreed with him. 'But—but I took his registration number.'

'His number? Why did you do that, Mr Arbuthnot?'

'I don't know, Chief Inspector. But when I got back to my flat I found I was reciting it to myself.'

'Second sight,' muttered Sester a trifle more loudly than he had intended.

'Certainly not, Sergeant,' said Mr Arbuthnot, hurt. 'I do occasionally find myself repeating a number or a phrase— an address, maybe—that I've noticed somewhere and it's stuck in my memory. I forget it soon enough, naturally. I'd certainly have forgotten the taxi's number by now, but when I heard on the radio about another killing I wrote it down.'

Arbuthnot felt in his pocket and produced a slip of paper. 'Here you are, Chief Inspector. It may be no use, but it might help to fit a piece into your puzzle.'

'Thank you very much, Mr Arbuthnot. I'm grateful to you. I only wish everyone was as observant as you are, and as helpful to the police. But I must ask you not to mention your information to anyone else.'

'Of course not, Chief Inspector,' said Mr Arbuthnot as he turned away.

'Maybe you should have thanked that wretched Wellington again, sir,' said Sester when they were getting into their car a few minutes later, 'as well as the old boy.'

Tansey laughed. 'You're probably right. But get on the phone and start them tracing the cab-driver. Let's hope Arbuthnot got the number right. If so, it might give us the identity of Harry Cranworth's mysterious lady-friend on a plate. When you've done that, I think we'll go and talk to Donald Brooke-Brown.'

In fact, it was Paul Gainsford they spoke to first. He was outside his mews house, cleaning his car yet again. He greeted the two officers formally but pleasantly, then suddenly swore.

'Damn! I've cut myself.'

He pulled a handkerchief out of the pocket of the old slacks he was wearing and wound it tightly round his hand. Blood began to seep through.

'You'd better attend to that,' said Tansey.

'Yes. I can't afford to waste the precious stuff—'

'Waste it? You're not a—'

'A hæmophiliac or something? Good God, no. I was only making a joke. It's just that I've got a blood donor appointment this afternoon.'

'Blood donor, are you? What group?'

Gainsford studied Tansey thoughtfully. 'My blood group? Now, I wonder why you asked me that, Chief Inspector? I can't claim there's any secret about it—or anything uncommon. In fact I'm "O" and Rh positive, just about the most usual—and useful—of all.'

By this time Alysia Gainsford had appeared at their front door, and on seeing the state of her husband's hand had chased him into the house. Then she said to Tansey, 'Do you want to talk to Paul—to us—Chief Inspector? If so, you'd better come in too. I'm just making some instant coffee.'

They accepted the invitation, but they learnt little from the Gainsfords. Alysia borrowed novels from the Marylebone Public Library, but had never used the Reference Room. Nevertheless, she claimed to know Gemma Fielding by sight, mainly because of the latter's style of dress, though she had never spoken to her. As for Paul, he belonged to the London Library which more than satisfied his needs.

However, Paul had heard Donald Brooke-Brown return home in the small hours that morning, and—as he said—couldn't help hearing a little of the altercation with the taxi-driver. But he had taken no action. 'I wanted no part of it,' he said honestly.

Next door Tansey and Sester were made less welcome. Mrs Brooke-Brown, who was looking old and tired, was nevertheless at first adamant in her refusal to let them in to see Donald. He was in bed and not feeling well.

'If he's really ill, we'll get a police doctor. Otherwise we must see—'

Mrs Brooke-Brown glared at the officers. 'You've got no right to suggest he's malingering, Chief Inspector. Considering what my boy has been through—'

'—we must see him, you know, Mrs Brooke-Brown,' Tansey interrupted her.

'Oh, very well!' she agreed at length. 'At least it'll get you off our doorstep. Come up to the sitting-room and I'll fetch him. I suppose it's because of this other girl who's been killed.'

She didn't wait for a reply, but hurried upstairs, letting them find their own way into the sitting-room. While they waited Tansey stared out of the window, but Sester prowled around. He picked up a photograph in a silver frame. It was of a group of men in uniform with their names and ranks printed beneath, and having studied it he took it across to his superior.

'D'you see this, sir? Colonel Ian Brooke-Brown with his regimental officers. He'd have had what they used to call a personal weapon, wouldn't he? I wonder if his son inherited it.'

'Possibly. A lot of people didn't hand them in when they should have done—and haven't done so since, in spite of the occasional amnesties.'

Sester scarcely had time to replace the photograph when Mrs Brooke-Brown returned with Donald. A short night had done nothing to improve Brooke-Brown's appearance. One eye was a brilliant black. His nose and mouth were swollen, so that the lisp due to his missing tooth was more apparent than ever. And there were long weals down his cheeks.

'You've met with an accident, Mr Brooke-Brown?' Tansey regarded him in surprise and had some difficulty in keeping his voice level.

'No. It was *not* an accident. I went to the cinema yesterday evening. I came out before the end of the film because it bored me, and I was set upon—mugged—by two youths and a girl. They left me unconscious in an alley, having stolen everything they could.'

'Where was all this? You reported it to the police, I imagine?' said Tansey.

'It happened in some alleyway in Soho. And I didn't report it. What could the police do? All I wanted was to get home as quickly as possible,' said Brooke-Brown.

He stopped speaking, and Tansey began his questions. Brooke-Brown remained typically vague and seemingly indifferent—attitudes which annoyed the Chief Inspector.

He said, 'You do realize, Mr Brooke-Brown, that last night, while you claim to have been lying in an unknown alley somewhere in Soho, another young woman was killed—garrotted, like your wife and Harry Cranworth's wife?'

'Yes, I know. My mother told me. She heard about it on the radio.'

'And that's all you've got to say?'

Brooke-Brown shrugged. 'This new girl means nothing to me—less than Jean Cranworth, because I knew Mrs Cranworth slightly. I don't believe I've ever in my life spoken to Miss—Miss Fielding, is it?'

'What's your blood group, Mr Brooke-Brown?'

'My blood group?' The sudden change in the line of inquiry seemed to agitate Brooke-Brown. 'My blood group? I—I don't know. I've no idea.'

'I see. Well, what about the clothes you were wearing last night. I'd like to have a look at them.'

'I've thrown them away,' Mrs Brooke-Brown said. 'They were torn and filthy and quite unwearable.'

'And bloodstained?' Tansey said. When there was no answer he added, 'Please fetch them, Mrs Brooke-Brown.'

White-faced, she went. Tansey felt sorry for her, but not for her son. While he continued with his questions and waited for the clothes to be brought he told himself that he mustn't let his judgement become clouded by Brooke-Brown's failure to make any effort on his own behalf—or any attempt to save his mother from at best considerable embarrassment.

Mrs Brooke-Brown returned with a pair of slacks and a

jacket. They were certainly torn and stained, but it was obvious that they had been expensive garments. They were not, Tansey thought at once, the clothes that someone would have chosen in which to pose as a delivery man. Nevertheless, he would take them—if nothing else, they would serve to confirm Brooke-Brown's blood group. He told Sester to prepare a receipt.

Neither of the Brooke-Browns spoke. They had become very still. When the Chief Inspector rose to go, and as usual thanked them for their help, their responses were automatic. Brooke-Brown remained seated and merely grunted and nodded; his mother showed them out, also with the minimum of words.

'They're scared, sir,' said Sester when he and Tansey were alone in their car.

'Maybe they have cause, Sergeant.'

'Sir?' It seemed to Sester as if the Chief Inspector was about to share his thoughts.

'Brooke-Brown's a pretty satisfying suspect in many ways,' Tansey said slowly. 'For instance, he could be right for the "why" of these murders. Yet somehow he doesn't quite fit the picture of a terrifying villain.'

Sester's face puckered into a frown, which made it look younger than ever. 'What do you mean by the "why", sir—the motive?'

'In a way. I'll try to explain,' said Tansey. 'One single motive can hardly fit all the crimes, unless . . .' He lapsed into silence.

'Sir?' queried Sester.

'As I was saying, it's hard to think of a single motive to fit them all, but at least it's a fair assumption that there's some logical connection between the women which might lead us to what I've called the "why", and it seems to me that the most obvious link is the Cranworths.'

'And Brooke-Brown admits that because of his wife and

her relationship with Harry Cranworth he hates Harry. He's even demonstrated it. He's no alibi for any of the nights in question. Surely he fits better than anyone, sir?'

'Perhaps—if we can establish some connection between him and Gemma Fielding—'

The car phone trilled, interrupting the conversation. Tansey took the receiver. He said very little, but listened for several minutes.

'Good!' he exclaimed at last, ending the call. 'Two items of interest, Sergeant. The local coppers have visited Gemma Fielding's mother. She says Gemma has made a will leaving everything she possessed to her two nieces, aged twelve and ten. So that rules out money as a motive. Not that we've ever thought of it in that sense in this case.'

'But it could be relevant to Catherine Brooke-Brown, sir,' Sester reminded Tansey.

'Yes. Though probably it only confuses the issue.' Tansey smiled wryly. 'The second item's more important. A motorbike's been found abandoned in the basement of an unoccupied house not far from Gemma Fielding's flat. A constable on the lookout for squatters spotted it. The number's been checked. The machine was reported stolen about a month ago, and they say it won't start. There's a newish stain on the saddle that might be blood. In addition a search revealed a helmet in a dustbin nearby. No obvious fingerprints on the bike or the helmet, which is odd in itself, but of course there'll be hairs and sweat and so on to work with.'

'More trouble for Forensic, sir.'

'Yes. We're keeping them busy. And we mustn't forget to arrange to send Brooke-Brown's clothes off for analysis. But first let's shift ourselves from this mews and go and look at the house where the bike and helmet were found.' Tansey gave Sester directions. 'The find may not be relevant, but I bet it is,' he added as they set off. 'What would you make of it, Sergeant?'

'Assuming it's our villain, sir, I'm wondering why he left them so close to the scene of the latest crime. You say the bike's not functioning?'

'So I'm told.'

'That could be the explanation. He wouldn't want to be seen in the vicinity wheeling a motorbike. He'd be much more noticeable than if he was riding it. Same goes for walking and carrying a helmet.'

'I was hoping you'd say he got rid of them because he no longer had any need for them.'

'There's that possibility too,' admitted Sester.

'Let's hope it's the right one,' said Tansey. 'Here we are, Sergeant, to judge by the uniformed man on guard and the tapes around the place. So let's be practical. We'll inspect the house, deal with Brooke-Brown's clothing and go and eat. I don't know about you, but I'm starving.'

CHAPTER 18

After a quick lunch in the Station canteen Detective Chief Inspector Tansey went to the incident room and collected a pile of files to study in the quiet of his office. He intended to commence a detailed review of the case. He read page after page of interrogation reports, notes on interviews, details from the scene of crime teams and the forensic experts—and, in particular, the measured, passionless prose of the pathologist who so far had conducted two PMs. These brought back to Tansey scenes he always wished he could forget—and reminded him that he would have to face another tomorrow—cold, tiled theatres where gowned and gloved doctors laid bare a body's inner secrets. They also reminded him of the horrific nature of the three deaths— made more unnerving by the fact that they had taken place in what should have been the safety of the young women's homes.

At one point the Chief Inspector rose and paced about his small room. He felt restless and useless. Inevitably, he was still lacking a great deal of information about the latest crime, he reflected—on the blood and tissue in Gemma Fielding's nails, for example, on any hair and sweat in the crash helmet, on the rose petal, on so many aspects of the affair. But he knew it was a waste of effort to attempt to put pressure on the scientists and technicians in the Met's Forensic Laboratory; he would be informed if and when any item of evidential value had been discovered. He knew he couldn't fault the efficiency or dedication of those working on the case.

His phone rang, and he leapt for it hopefully. He was not totally disappointed. The taxi-driver who had delivered Harry Cranworth to Manchester Square about six-thirty that morning had been traced. But apparently he had been driving his cab till after nine a.m., and his wife was steadfastly refusing to wake him—murders or no murders. She would make sure he called Chief Inspector Tansey as soon as he surfaced.

Tansey swore, but the officer who had made the initial call at the driver's home had remarked that the woman seemed patently honest and the Chief Inspector hadn't the heart to blame her for causing a slight delay by defending her husband's right to rest. He put down the receiver, and the phone rang again immediately. This time the news was better still. A plastic bag had been unearthed in a dustbin, not far from where the motorbike had been found. The bag contained the remains of what had undoubtedly been half a dozen pink roses. A further search of the contents of dustbins in the vicinity had produced a long box of the type in which flowers were often packed. It had been torn into small pieces, and the name on the lid defaced, but one

fragment had seemingly escaped attention. This had revealed part of a phone number, which had been traced to
a flower shop in Chelsea.

All this sounded simple, and was indeed routine, but
Tansey was quite aware of the painstaking, detailed and—
in the case of the dustbin searches—unpleasant work that
lay behind the facts. He decided to leave instructions about
the taxi-driver and go to Chelsea himself. It was an excellent
excuse to escape from the confines of the Station and his
fruitless belabouring of the files. He called for Sester.

'Great, sir,' agreed the sergeant as they set off. 'I wanted
to get out myself.'

Tansey grinned. 'It's all in the cause of duty, Sergeant,'
he said. 'At least it gives us an illusion that we're being
active,' he added sombrely.

'We're not doing too badly, sir. Miss Fielding was only
found this morning, and we do seem to be getting some
breaks.'

'Yes,' said Tansey, and thought that any breaks were
largely due to a lack of efficiency on the part of the villain,
rather than to any brilliance on his own part. In any case,
this seemed to be the first occasion on which the villain had
left some pointers for the police.

But why, Tansey asked himself, having committed two
perfect crimes, had he made such a mess of the third? Jean
Cranworth and Catherine Brooke-Brown had both been
small women and easy to overcome, but anyone with the
merest acquaintance with Gemma Fielding should have
expected her to put up a spirited fight for her life. It was
fanciful, Tansey speculated, but it was almost as if, for some
as yet unknown reason, the killer had been mentally, if not
physically, overwhelmed by her personality, even when she
was dead. Had she meant that much more to him than his
earlier victims?

We still don't know enough about these women, Tansey

thought. Fielding must have had lovers before Steve Cranworth. One of them might have resented being cast aside
for Steve. And what about Jean? Someone might have
wanted her, even if she hadn't wanted him. As for Catherine
Brooke-Brown, presumably someone had supplanted Harry
in her varied love-life—whoever had been with her at the
Richmond cottage the night that Harry's wife was killed. It
was not surprising that, in spite of public appeals, no one had
come forward to claim the honour, but a pity that neither
the Cranworths nor the inquisitive Paul Gainsford had any
ideas. Police efforts had totally failed to trace Catherine's
partner that night. The Chief Inspector continued to pon-
der.

Chelsea was busy on a Saturday afternoon—with people
shopping, window-gazing, chatting with friends on street
corners, and with traffic. The King's Road was one long
jam. Parking, of course, was a matter of luck.

Sergeant Sester would have parked on a yellow line
directly in front of Veronica's, the flower shop in a turning
off the main road which announced its name in a bright
blue script on its white fascia, but Tansey wished to avoid
drawing attention to themselves. After driving around for
some minutes, the sergeant managed to sneak into a place,
ahead of a hesitant driver who was contemplating the difficulty of reversing into the slot.

When they reached the shop, which was heavy with the
scent of flowers and plants, there were two or three customers being served. A lady was discussing with an assistant
how to nurture an orange tree, while her husband was
inspecting some cacti suspiciously. A young man seemed to
be having difficulty with the wording of the card he wished
to attach to a mixed bunch he was sending to someone—
almost certainly a girlfriend—and a pretty, plump woman
in her forties was helping him. The officers waited patiently.

The young man departed, and the woman turned to Tansey and Sester. 'Sorry to have kept you,' she said pleasantly.

'That's all right,' said Tansey. 'But I'm afraid we're not customers. You remember that a police officer phoned earlier about some pink roses. We're following up that call.' He kept his voice low and silently passed the woman his card. 'Are you "Veronica" or is that a—'

'A trade name? No.' She laughed. 'I'm Veronica White. And, after all, there are flowers called veronicas. This is my shop. My daughter and I live in the flat above.' She looked at Tansey and Sester doubtfully for a moment, then said, 'You'd better come into the back room.'

They followed her through an archway concealed by a beaded curtain into a room where a girl in her teens, a young version of Veronica White, was packing orders on a large table. In spite of the signs of disorder, a tap dripping into a sink, the floor covered with cuttings, boxes piled precariously on the only chair and flowers and fern everywhere, it was clearly a businesslike operation.

'My daughter, Sandra,' said Veronica White unnecessarily. 'She's the one who'll be able to help you, if anyone can, though I really don't understand—' To her daughter she added, 'This is a Detective Chief Inspector—' she looked at the card in her hand—'Tansey, from Marylebone, with—'

'Detective-Sergeant Sester,' supplied the sergeant.

'They've come about the man who bought the last of those roses,' said Mrs White.

Sandra was eyeing Tansey. 'A Detective Chief Inspector,' she said. 'That man's done something serious, then?'

'We don't know yet,' Tansey said. 'Perhaps you'll be able to help us find out. First, tell us about those roses. You must sell a lot of flowers. Why should you remember these in particular?'

'They were a special order for a wedding anniversary,'
the girl explained. 'Thirty deep pink roses. Hot-house, of
course, at this time of year, and unbelievably expensive.
Anyway, our wholesalers got the order wrong and sent us
three dozen. They're very good as a rule, and helpful if we
ask for something in a hurry, so we didn't want to send the
odd half-dozen back. But because they were so expensive
they didn't sell. At least, not until this chap bought
them.'

She paused for breath, and Tansey smiled at her encouragingly. 'Yes. I can see why you remember them—and
him, I hope. A bit of luck for us.'

'There won't be any trouble, will there?' asked Mrs White
suddenly. 'I mean, we'd had them a couple of days and they
were a bit tired. So we put some stuff in the water to pep
them up. A lot of florists do that sort of thing all the time,
but we try not to. It isn't really fair, only in this case—'

'Don't be silly, Mum,' Sandra interrupted. 'Detective
Chief Inspectors have better things to do than chase dishonest florists.'

'We're not dishonest, dear. I was just explaining—'

'Anyway, this guy deserved to be taken.' Sandra gave
Tansey a winning grin. 'He breezed into the shop two days
ago, on Thursday afternoon, looked around, and said, "I'll
take those roses" without a please or thank you. I pointed
out that they weren't cheap, but he just got out his wallet
and put a twenty-pound note on top of the till.'

'Have you still got the note?' Tansey asked quickly.

'Oh no. We take our cash to the bank every day,' said
Mrs White.

'He asked for the flowers to be put in a box,' Sandra
continued, 'but he refused a card. He said he'd be delivering
them personally.'

'Now, can you describe him, Miss White?' Tansey felt
certain he knew how the flowers had been delivered.

'About as tall as you are. Beige raincoat, with the collar turned up. Cap pulled well down. I couldn't see his hair.' Sandra White was observant. She frowned. 'I was alone in the shop. I had to pack the roses, and he kept moving about. But he had a pointed nose. I remember that, and his hands. He wore gloves all the time, though it wasn't cold.'

Tansey nodded at Sester, who produced a small sheaf of photographs, mostly from police files, but a couple thanks to the press. He made a place for them on the table among broken flowers and leaves, and spread them out. Sandra White studied them carefully.

'I'm trying to imagine them in a cap, with their shoulders hunched up a bit,' she said, 'but it's difficult.'

'Take your time, Miss White.'

'Definitely none of these.' She pushed four away from her. 'And neither of these two. They're a couple of good-looking chaps, and awfully alike. Are they brothers?'

'Yes,' said Tansey briefly as she relegated Harry and Steve Cranworth to the discards.

'It could be him,' she said at last, 'but I'm not sure, by any means. He just looks the most likely to me.'

'Thanks anyway,' said Tansey.

The photograph that Sandra White had chosen was of Donald Brooke-Brown.

Bob Spruce did not share Sandra White's uncertainty. Spruce was the taxi-driver whom Mr Arbuthnot had seen delivering Harry Cranworth at his house in Manchester Square that morning—surprisingly, it was still Saturday, Tansey remembered.

'Of course I'm sure, Chief Inspector,' said Spruce when Tansey, on returning to Seymour Street, was able to speak to him on the phone. 'I know that Terrace like I know my own street. I'd just set down this fare—a youngish couple, it was—at—' he gave the number of the building, which

the Chief Inspector recognized—'and the man was putting
his key in the lock of the main door. I was about to drive
off when there was a shout, and I saw a second gent open
an iron gate and come out of the alley between this block
and the next. He hurried towards me and I took him to
Manchester Square. He gave me a good tip and that's all I
can tell you.'

'Did you see anyone else in Manchester Square?' Tansey
asked, in an effort to test the reliability of the witness's
recollections.

'Yes, I did. An old chap walking a little dog—a poodle,
I think,' said Spruce. 'And a big Mercedes passed me going
round the Square.'

Mr Spruce, Tansey thought, was both accurate and con-
vincing. The Chief Inspector thanked him for the information he'd provided, and said goodbye after arranging a
date for an officer to take a formal statement. Then Tansey
sat for a few moments staring straight in front of him and
wondering how to play his next card. He owed Harry
Cranworth nothing. Harry had lied and lied again and
wasted a lot of time. Nevertheless . . . He reached for the
telephone. But there was no answer from either of the
Cranworths' numbers.

Almost reluctantly he tapped out another number, which
he was sure would produce some response. He was right; a
voice answered at once, 'Mr Hector Greyling's residence.'
Tansey gave his name and rank and asked to speak to
Greyling.

'Mr Greyling is not at home at present, sir,' was the reply.
'He may be back late tonight or tomorrow morning.'

'Then let me speak to Mrs Greyling, please,' said Tansey,
relieved that he wouldn't have to deal with an irate and
probably sceptical husband.

When Pamela Greyling eventually came to the phone he
gave her no time to speak. He said at once, 'Mrs Greyling,

it's essential I talk to you. I'll be with you in about twenty minutes.' When she began to protest he added, 'It won't take long, and it's for your own sake.' He put down his receiver before she could argue further.

And within twenty minutes, in spite of the heavy Saturday afternoon traffic, Tansey was shown into the Greylings' imposing drawing-room. He was alone. It had been agreed that Sester should remain in their car.

Mrs Greyling greeted him coldly. She gestured him to a chair, but didn't offer to shake hands. She was wearing a simple violet-coloured wool dress that even Tansey could see at once was an expensive model, and there was no denying that she was beautiful. For a split second Tansey envied Harry Cranworth.

Speaking softly he said, 'Mrs Greyling, last night another young woman was garrotted. I'm not saying her life could have been saved, but police time and effort that should have been spent finding her murderer has been wasted over the past weeks by individuals telling lies and half-lies, for reasons they mistakenly thought were justified.'

As Tansey paused, Pamela Greyling said, 'So what's all this got to do with me? I don't understand, Chief Inspector. I've never lied to you.'

'No, Mrs Greyling, but you've let Harry Cranworth lie on your behalf, haven't you? You could have given him an alibi for the night his wife was killed, but you've let the police continue to suspect him. What's more, the same is true of last night, when Miss Fielding was killed.'

'I—I don't know what you're talking about. I shall—'

'You'll what, Mrs Greyling? Tell your husband?'

'Yes! No! Oh my God, Harry swore he'd never—'

'And he's kept his word to you. But as far as I'm concerned that's what caused the trouble. In any case, he was seen leaving the private garden entrance to your flat early this morning.'

Pamela Greyling began to sob. 'I've been mad—mad to take such risks. But I met Harry at a party—and he was attractive and attentive, while Hector was busy with his high-powered contacts . . .'

She paused, while Tansey waited.

'It always seemed safe enough,' she went on eventually. 'We were very careful. Harry used the side gate so that he never met any of the other residents of this building, and he left early before the staff were around.'

She hesitated again, while Tansey waited silently, and then continued in a rush of words. 'Now Hector'll never forgive me. I'm not just a wife to him. In a way, I'm a possession. And he'll imagine his colleagues, his acquaintances—he doesn't have friends—all laughing at him. He'll never believe that since I married him there's been no one else but Harry. And he'll find means to ruin Harry. He's very powerful. You won't credit what he's done—'

'Mrs Greyling, please!' Tansey interrupted her firmly. 'If you can give Harry Cranworth alibis for the two nights in question, which I'm sure you can, we'll consider the matter closed unless something unforeseen turns up.'

'You mean Hector won't have to know?' Immediately her tears ceased.

'At least the police won't inform him,' said Tansey, wishing he could sound less pompous. 'But I can't answer for your household. Surely—'

'Marie, the housekeeper—she knows. It wouldn't have been possible without her.'

'Then she'll support what you say—about Harry? For my own satisfaction, I mean.'

'Yes, Chief Inspector. Shall I send for her?'

'Please. But not immediately.'

Ten minutes later Mrs Greyling was drying her eyes as she crossed the room to ring the bell for the housekeeper, and in another ten Marie was showing Tansey from the flat.

He was well satisfied with the interview but, oddly enough, he was surprised to find that nearly all his sympathy was now with Hector Greyling.

CHAPTER 19

'I'm so sorry I've got to leave you today, darling, but I must attend Gemma Fielding's PM. A great deal may depend on what the medics—and the forensic chaps—come up with.'

'Don't be silly, Dick. I'll be fine. I intend to spend a nice quiet Sunday reading and watching the telly. I'm only sorry that my being unwell kept us awake half the night.'

Dick Tansey had just brought Hilary her breakfast in bed. He was worried about her, and about the baby. Had it been an ordinary day at his Kidlington headquarters he would have been able to arrange for someone to stand in for him. Here in London, in his position with the Met and at such an important point in a triple murder investigation, such a step was impossible. But in the circumstances it was doubly unfortunate that Hilary was having a difficult pregnancy.

'You're sure you don't mind, Hilary?'

'Quite sure. Please don't worry about me, Dick. You've got enough on your mind at present. Just think—if they can prove the blood under poor Gemma's nails is the same odd type as Steve Cranworth's, you'd probably have enough evidence to take him in, wouldn't you?'

'That's too much to hope for. It's much more likely to be a common group—"O", like Brooke-Brown and half of London, for instance. No, I've got a feeling they'll have to go in for some much more complicated blood and tissue typing if we're to get anything out of Gemma's fight with her attacker.'

Tansey sighed. 'You know, Hilary, the more I think about this case—these murders—the more worried I become at the lack of evidence pointing in any single direction. There are too few suspects so far, and none of them seems to fill the bill exactly. But, to my mind, there's one connecting thread—the Cranworth brothers. After all, the victims were the wife of one brother, the girlfriend or ex-girlfriend of the same brother and another woman—the girlfriend of the second brother. That can't be coincidence. At the very least, it looks as if someone had it in for the pair of them.'

'So—' said Hilary.

'So who have we got? Donald Brooke-Brown? He has an obvious motive—jealousy of a kind—but he seems to have accepted his wife's previous infidelities without going off the handle.'

'But he did attack Harry?'

'I know. In a way, that's another point that's arguably in his favour. I can't believe that anyone—in the course of a series of horrific murders—would take time off to mount such a secondary effort. Can you?'

'No. I suppose not.'

'Then the Gainsfords—they represent a bit of an enigma. But it's hard to find a motive for them—'

'What about the Cranworths themselves?'

'I've thought of them, of course. Steve, incidentally, has a motorcycle licence, though he claims he hasn't been on a bike for years. I've even thought of some complex plot devised by one of Gemma's previous lovers. But Steve's been fairly frank about this, I think, and he says that he had no immediate predecessor whom he'd replaced. The man had merely emigrated to Australia, and he and Gemma seem to have parted on good terms, as far as any-one knows.'

'So—' said Hilary again.

'So we've got to face the fact that we're looking for

someone new—someone who hasn't entered into our calculations so far. And that's a depressing notion.'

'Suppose,' began Hilary, 'that you're right about the killer having it in for the Cranworths—to such an extent that he wants to inflict some kind of vengeance or retribution on them because one of them has—or had—the girl he wants or wanted. It's hard to imagine Jean in that role—she was pleasant, but not especially exciting—and it's hard to imagine anyone taking an affaire with Catherine Brooke-Brown seriously enough to do murder for it. If there's anything in your assumption, the girl in question must be Gemma.'

There was a series of soft thuds in the hall outside the flat. 'That'll be Mrs Meade delivering the newspapers,' Hilary said. 'The Sundays are far too fat to go through the letter-boxes. Be a dear, Dick, and fetch ours.'

'OK. But I'll put your tray out first, and give the bossy Mrs Meade time to make herself scarce.'

Hilary laughed. She thought with pleasure of a lazy morning in bed studying the papers. She didn't envy Dick attending an autopsy, and probably working late. She felt tired but quite well now, and decided that she was something of a fraud. If it became a sunny afternoon she might go for a short walk in Regent's Park.

Tansey returned carrying the *Sunday Times* and let its bulk drop on the bed beside Hilary. 'That should keep you busy,' he said. 'And what's the matter with David Horner?'

'Why?'

'Well, he's usually quite a friendly chap, but this morning when I opened our front door he was picking up his paper, too. Instead of saying good morning he grabbed it and bobbed back inside as fast as he could. Admittedly he was wearing pyjamas and a dressing-gown, but still—'

'Perhaps he still looks awful, and was ashamed to let you see him.' Hilary was amused.

Her husband stared at her. 'What on earth are you talking about?' he demanded.

'Oh, I forgot to tell you. It's only gossip. Natalie Smythe went to a party on Friday night. A friend brought her back and they were sitting outside in the car when David Horner came along. According to Natalie, he was none too steady on his feet, and he looked as if he'd been in a fight.'

'Perhaps he'd been to a party too.'

'Perhaps. But I shouldn't think he's much of a drinker normally. Natalie said she'd never seen him even mildly tight before.'

'He should have got over it by now, anyway.' Tansey glanced at the clock. 'Darling, I must go. Sester'll be downstairs, and I don't want to keep him waiting. I'll call you if I get a chance and I'll get home as early as I can.'

'All right, but don't worry about me,' Hilary repeated. 'And I may go out for a walk if the weather's reasonable.' She lifted her face as he bent to kiss her. 'I hope you have a good day, Dick.'

To suggest that Chief Inspector Tansey forgot his wife the moment he slipped into the police car beside Sergeant Sester would be unfair. But she remained only on the edge of his mind, and once he was in the mortuary observing the PM on Gemma Fielding's body and listening to the pathologist, who was fully prepared to carry on a conversation as he carried out his somewhat macabre activities, he was wholly concentrated on what he was hearing.

'. . . the first point is that she was shot first; the garrotting came later,' the doctor was saying. 'I'm certain of that. And you'll be pleased to hear we've been doing quite a lot of work in the lab overnight on your behalf. I think we may have solved the problem of the excessive amount of blood. It looks as if the attacker had an epistasis—'

'A what?'

'A nose-bleed. There's a good deal of what looks like nasal mucus mixed with the blood, and there are no signs that it came from the victim.'

'I see,' said Tansey thoughtfully. 'And what about the blood type?'

'Not terribly helpful yet. The blood that we assume came from this bleed was Group "O" and Rh positive, like Fielding herself.' The pathologist shrugged. 'We can do some more complex typing to make sure, but I thought we'd wait to see you turn up samples from any suspects to compare it with. And don't forget the tissue under her nails, either. We've got plenty of that to make comparisons and convince a jury—at least I hope so. The trouble is we need a few suspects.'

'I'm quite aware of that,' said Tansey shortly, and thought that their unusual blood now seemed to have put both the Cranworths in the clear.

'Would you like me to tell you how I'd interpret the medical and forensic evidence at the present stage? If you promise not to hold me to it, I'll tell you what I think happened.'

'I wish you would.' Tansey never minded picking other experts' brains.

'Right. I've finished here. My assistant can clear up, so let's get out of this place. I'll wash up and we'll go along to the office. A little more pleasant perhaps?' He grinned at the Chief Inspector, showing his discoloured teeth. 'I know, I know. People never get used to it. I'm not entirely sure I have myself. Still, it's a job that's got to be done.'

Minutes later, over cups of coffee in the mortuary office, the pathologist continued his exposition. 'Most of this'll be in my report, but I won't put my guesses on paper. So, I repeat, don't hold me to any of them at present. I can just see learned counsel making hay of me.'

'I won't,' promised Tansey, wondering, like so many

others before him, how pathologists managed to remain so cheerful.

'OK. Well, I suspect that as soon as Fielding opened the door of her flat she recognized the man, and probably recognized him as an unwelcome visitor—someone she didn't like. Perhaps some gesture betrayed him. At any rate, it's possible the lassie divined what he had in mind, and her reactions were quick. She went for him. She tore at his face —hence the blood and tissue under her nails—and she hit him in the nose.'

'Would she have knocked out any teeth?' Tansey asked, thinking of Brooke-Brown.

'That point occurred to me, and I examined her hands and knuckles carefully. It's not conclusive, of course, but there are no abrasions of the kind you might expect if she hit something sharp like a tooth, rather than a soft nose. Anyway, faced with this sudden attack, our villain produced a gun, and shot her at close range. We've got the round. I'm no expert, but it wasn't at all badly deformed and at a glance I'd call it a .38; the entry and exit wounds would support that, too. A Smith & Wesson, perhaps—they're pretty common, I gather?'

'That's true.' Tansey nodded. 'Left over from military service somewhere, presumably.'

'Exactly. Well, then the man started to pull her along to the bedroom, but his nose was acting up. So he stopped. But he took time to garrotte her, presumably in order to link her with the other two murders. You could say garrotting's a kind of trademark of his.' The pathologist laughed.

Tansey was in no mood for laughter, and merely grunted. 'Anything else?'

'The timing, which'll be in my report. The lassie was killed between ten at night and two in the morning approximately. She'd had a light supper about eight.

Incidentally, she wasn't pregnant, and there had been no attempt to molest her, sexually or otherwise—apart of course from killing her twice, as it were.'

'Now, what about the motorbike and the helmet?'

'The stain on the bike is blood. Group "O" again, which isn't much immediate help in finding a suspect, I guess. But the typing and a comparison of hair and sweat in the helmet with traces—especially of hair we found in Fielding's flat —suggest that the helmet and the bike belonged to the murderer. All we need is the chap—though there's always a good chance that an expert witness for the defence could put enough doubt in the minds of a jury to—'

'Try not to encourage me, will you?' said Tansey sarcastically. He was beginning to feel he'd had enough of this pathologist and his seemingly casual approach to the case.

'All right,' the doctor replied. 'It's par for the course, as you know only too well, I'm sure. But I'll give you one item of information that's definite. It may surprise you.' He sounded triumphant.

'What's that?' Tansey was forced to ask.

'Those clothes you brought in—torn, dirty, bloody. I'm not asking where you got them, but they didn't belong to the chap who killed Fielding.'

'You're sure? A hundred per cent?'

'In this business I'm never sure of anything a hundred per cent. But say ninety-nine.' Again he laughed. 'I ought to be a GP. Say ninety-nine, indeed. It's like this,' he went on, 'the blood shows major differences. There are no hairs on the suit that match anything in the flat, either, and . . .'

The pathologist went into some further technical details, but Tansey had ceased to listen; he would wait for the report to glean any other evidence. He had other thoughts on his mind.

*

'So it looks as if we're back where we started, doesn't it, sir?' commented Sergeant Sester dolefully when they had returned to the Incident Room at Seymour Street.

'Not necessarily,' said Tansey slowly. 'Not quite, anyway. For one thing I've got a much clearer picture of the type we're after. It was my wife who put the idea into my head. He could be someone who knew Gemma Fielding, though probably not well, and who wanted her as a lover. That could be why he hated Steve Cranworth—and, by association, Harry Cranworth. And when he couldn't have Gemma Fielding he decided to kill her.'

'But what about—'

'Wait, Sergeant. This is a bit of a leap in the dark, but suppose our villain planned to hide the identity of his intended victim by killing other women—women connected with the Cranworths in order to involve them—and on the principle that the best place to hide a book is in a library.' He stopped abruptly.

'We must pay more attention to that public library where she worked,' he said at length. 'After all, it's where she spent most of her time. I remembered that Steve Cranworth mentioned what he called the "Faithfuls", who spent most of their time in the Reference Department, too. I've been wondering . . .'

It was, of course, Sunday, so the library was closed, but the staff had been interviewed the previous day. Once again Tansey went through the relevant files, but many telephone calls later he found he wasn't much further advanced. Of the two characters whom Gemma Fielding had called nuisances, the man who was constantly claiming her attention by asking abstruse questions could not possibly be the villain. He had been in hospital for the last ten days with a perforated appendix.

The other wasn't so often in the library, and no one but Steve Cranworth seemed to have noticed him particularly.

'All I know is what Gemma told me,' Steve said somewhat irritably when Tansey phoned. 'There was this accident. Gemma was on her motorbike in the High Street and had to brake sharply because an old girl had suddenly started across a pedestrian crossing. There was a patch of wet tarmac, and the bike skidded sideways. This guy picked Gemma up, and the bike, and was duly solicitous. The old girl was untouched—not even shaken.'

'When was this, Mr Cranworth?'

'About a year ago, before Gemma and I really got together. Chief Inspector, for all I know the good Samaritan chap ceased to fancy Gemma when she made it clear he wasn't going to get anywhere with her.'

'But what *did* she say about him?' Tansey persisted. 'What did she call him? Did she say he was tall or short? Did she give him a name, even?'

Steve Cranworth laughed. 'She called him, "Clammy Hands", if you really want to know. I remember her saying he wasn't bad-looking, but that his clammy hands revolted her.'

Clammy hands! The phrase instantly reminded Tansey of Natalie Smythe. He had been amused by Hilary's story of the pass David Horner had made at Natalie, and her comment about his hands. Of course, there were hundreds —thousands—of men in London with clammy hands. But men who by their own admission had frequented the Reference Department of the Marylebone Public Library? Men who had come home in the early hours of Saturday morning, seemingly drunk and looking as if they'd been in a fight? Men who had lost interest in a fiancée about a year ago, when possibly they had met someone 'interesting and vibrant'? He'd heard those adjectives before, and certainly they described Gemma Fielding.

'Chief Inspector! Are you there?'

'Sorry, Mr Cranworth. I—I was ruminating. Are you

sure you never heard Miss Fielding call this chap David—
or—Donald or something?'

'Absolutely positive. Look, I'm giving you the wrong
impression. Gemma didn't talk about this man all the time.
I doubt if she mentioned him to me more than three or four
times altogether.'

'Did she ever point him out to you?'

'Now you remind me, yes, she did. Once. We passed him
in the High Street one day. In fact, that was when she told
me the story of her little contretemps, and the subsequent
attentions of "Clammy Hands".'

'So how would you describe him?'

'It was raining, and he had his collar turned up. Besides,
he'd gone on before I had any reason to be interested.'

'You must have got some impression of him. Short? Tall?
Fat? Thin?'

'OK,' Steve Cranworth replied resignedly. 'As I recall,
he was about your height, brown hair, neither fat nor thin,
athletic—he was walking fast, swinging along—and I think
he had a pointed nose.'

'Are you joking?' Tansey was immediately suspicious
about these details, though Sandra White from the flower
shop had said the man who bought the roses had a pointed
nose.

'About the nose, yes, perhaps, but not the rest. Sorry I
can't do better, Chief Inspector.'

'You've done well enough. Thanks a lot, Mr Cranworth.'

For several minutes after he had put down the receiver
Dick Tansey sat with his head in his hands. He could
make out a case against David Horner, but it was entirely
circumstantial and less strong than the one he had prepared
against Donald Brooke-Brown—and that had been demolished by the scientists. Nevertheless, the idea must be pur-
sued, and in the meantime—

Hilary! The Chief Inspector thought of his wife, alone in

the flat opposite David Horner, who might—just might—
be a cunning and cold-blooded killer. The idea was enough
to make Dick Tansey feel physically ill. There was only one
answer. He would go home at once, make Hilary pack a
bag and take her down to her parents for a few days. They
would be happy to have her, and she would be safe. He
could cope by himself. And it shouldn't be for long. With
all the information the forensic boys had been able to gather
about the villain, it shouldn't be difficult to clear Horner,
who might well turn out to bear no resemblance to Gemma
Fielding's 'Clammy Hands'.

Of course it was a potentially embarrassing situation.
Tansey told himself that he would have to move very
carefully. If his suspicions were right, so be it. But if they
proved wrong, he couldn't avoid mortally offending the
Horners. He and Hilary would be gone in a few months,
but Detective Chief Inspector Porter and his family would
continue to have them as close neighbours.

But to hell with any potential embarrassment, Tansey
thought. This mattered—really mattered. He'd wasted
enough time already. First, he must get Hilary safely away.
Then he would look into David Horner—and seriously. He
went in search of Sergeant Sester.

CHAPTER 20

If it had not been for an enterprising journalist, a freelance
anxious to make a name for himself, the safe and cautious
plan which Detective Chief Inspector Tansey had devised
might have worked. But chance, in the person of the journalist, frustrated it.

In their flat Hilary Tansey had made herself a ham salad
for lunch and was enjoying a cup of tea, when the doorbell

rang. She had decided to be lazy and avoid exercise; it was a sunny day, but there was a chill wind which deterred her.

The bell rang again. Hilary assumed that it was one of her neighbours, either Natalie Smythe or Mrs Horner, or possibly David. She couldn't imagine anyone else who would ring her doorbell in the middle of a Sunday afternoon —especially without warning from the entry-phone downstairs. Reluctantly she abandoned her tea, and went into the hall. Without bothering about the chain, she opened the door.

The man on the doorstep was a total stranger to her. He was in his mid-thirties, dark-haired, with a pink complexion and a forceful jaw. He was wearing grey slacks and a brown sweater over a green shirt and under an open raincoat. His smile was wide and not unattractive. Hilary's first impression was that he had come to the wrong flat.

'Yes?' she said. 'Who do you want?'

'You're Mrs Tansey? Mrs Richard Tansey?'

Hilary nodded. She swallowed hard. For one dreadful moment she thought that Dick had been hurt and this man had been sent to tell her. Then common sense reasserted itself. The police always did their best to break bad news gently, especially if it concerned one of their own. The Met would never have sent a young man alone on such an errand.

'Who are you?' she said coldly. 'What do you want? And how did you get into the building?'

'Oh, that was no problem—I just came in with a tenant, and I knew you were living in the Porters' flat. I've been here once before, to see him. I want to have a talk with you, Mrs Tansey. Perhaps I could come in and we could have a little chat. You know the kind of things people are interested in—what it's like to be married to a famous detective, how different the Met is from the Thames Valley Force—that sort of thing—'

Hilary stared at her visitor. 'You're a journalist!' she said
at length in some disgust. 'Why didn't you say so to start
with? Anyway, I don't give interviews.'

'Oh, come on, Mrs Tansey.' She had attempted to shut
the door, but he had been too quick for her and had jammed
his foot in the opening. 'I don't write for some scurrilous
rag, you know. My piece would be for a serious periodical,
the kind that doesn't print personal rubbish.'

'I don't care who you are! Or what sort of thing you write!
I don't wish to give an interview! Please go away and stop
bothering me.'

'Mrs Tansey, don't be silly. All I'm asking for is a few
minutes of your time. I promise you'll see a proof of my
copy before it's published.'

As he spoke he began to lean more heavily against the
door, and Hilary knew she wouldn't be able to hold her
position much longer. In ordinary circumstances she could
have dealt with the man easily. After all, she was a trained
police officer. But the circumstances were not normal, for
the baby inhibited her. She was fearful that any violent
physical movement might harm it.

'If you don't go at once, I shall scream,' she said calmly.
'These are friendly flats. Some of my neighbours will appear
at once, and they'll call the police.'

'Mrs Tansey, there's no need—'

'There's every need if you don't stop—'

It was hard to describe afterwards exactly what happened
at this point. Hilary may have released the pressure she was
putting on the door. The journalist may have shifted his
weight. But suddenly, for one reason or the other, the door
burst open and the man fell into the hall, and Hilary, pushed
aside and off balance, fell on top of him. She screamed, loud
and long.

The result was exactly what she would have hoped
for had she really been grappling with an attacker.

Within seconds David Horner appeared, followed almost immediately by his mother, and shortly afterwards by Natalie Smythe in a towelling robe, her hair spiky with shampoo.

David leapt forward and helped Hilary to her feet, delivering her into the supporting arms of his mother. He then stood over the man menacingly.

'What is it?' David demanded. 'What happened?'

'Are you hurt?' said his mother abruptly. Hilary couldn't help noticing that Mrs Horner seemed unusually tense and nervous, but she put that down to the shock of hearing screams.

'Are you all right, Hilary? What happened? Who is that man? Shall I call the police?' This from Natalie.

The journalist got to his feet. 'There's no need for anything like that,' he said angrily. 'I'm going. I was only trying to get some material for a magazine article. It's not a major crisis. It's not even a minor one. Or a crime. I'm sorry. Forget it,' he added to Hilary.

He pushed past David Horner and ran down the stairs. They heard the front door slam. By now the whole affair had become something of an anti-climax. Clearly Hilary was unharmed, and in retrospect the incident seemed stupidly trivial. Nevertheless, Hilary started to thank the Horners and Natalie Smythe for coming to her help so promptly, and to apologize for disturbing them, though Natalie was already returning to her interrupted hair-washing, and Mrs Horner was urging David back to their flat. Hilary found herself staring at his face, at the lacerated cheeks and the swollen nose.

'You look as if you've been in the wars, David,' she said as he watched her studying him.

'So he has, the poor boy,' said Mrs Horner. 'He went out yesterday evening and he was mugged on the way home.'

'*Yesterday* evening?' Hilary spoke without thinking. And

she was again aware of David's eyes fixed on her as if he
were trying to penetrate her thoughts.

'Three youths, they were,' Mrs Horner said at once.
'David's strong, but he couldn't stand any chance against
three of them. They beat him up and stole his wallet.'

But not his very expensive watch, Hilary thought at once,
catching sight of it on his wrist. 'Well, I—I'm glad it was
no worse,' she said quickly as her police training came to
the fore. 'I'm sure you reported it.'

'No, we didn't,' said Mrs Horner. She hesitated. Then,
'Saturday's a particularly bad night for this sort of thing,
as you know, and David said not to bother.'

She stopped, and Hilary was about to comment when she
continued, repeating what she had said so many times
before. 'It's dreadful how much violence there is about and,
with all respect to Mr Tansey, the police never seem to
catch the perpetrators.'

David had already returned to the Horners' flat, and
Hilary was no longer listening to his mother's worried
chatter. She made an excuse as soon as she could, shut her
front door and, thankful to be alone, leant against it. She
told herself that she was crazy. There had to be a simple
explanation for Mrs Horner's lie.

Because she had lied, deliberately. On the face of it, it
was unlikely that David had been mugged; muggers would
almost certainly have taken his watch. And the incident—
the mugging—or could it be something more sinister?—
had definitely not taken place on Saturday night, as the
Horners claimed. Natalie Smythe had seen David looking
as if he'd been in a drunken brawl, on *Friday* night. Yet Mrs
Horner had been at pains to stress that her son's injuries
had been inflicted on Saturday.

Why? Hilary asked herself. Could the reason conceivably
be that she was afraid her son David might be connected
with the killing of Gemma Fielding? It was a fact that David

knew Gemma; he was often in the library. And his face!
Dick had told her how Gemma had fought to save her life.

I really am crazy, Hilary thought. David Horner was
surely a good, kind man. A few minutes ago he had been
first on the scene to help her when she had screamed. His
mother always spoke of him with love and pride. What
possible motive could he have for killing three young women
in cold blood?

Nevertheless, Hilary was not a detective officer for nothing; she knew that two points needed explanation—the
strong possibility that the mugging was fictitious, and the
very obvious lies about its date.

She pulled herself away from the door and, going into the
sitting-room, collected her half-drunk cup of tea. It was cold
and unappetizing and, though she knew she was meant to
avoid too much caffeine, she decided to make herself a fresh
pot.

It was an hour later. Hilary had enjoyed her tea, and after
some cogitation had decided against calling Seymour Street
and trying to contact Dick. She hoped he would phone her,
as he had promised to try to do. If not, there would be time
enough to tell him what had happened when she saw him
later.

In fact by now, comfortable and relaxed and engrossed
in her knitting and an old movie on television, she had
managed to push the Horners and her nagging suspicions
into the back of her mind. Then she heard the sound that
in the last few weeks she had grown to know so well, the
key turning in the lock at the door of the flat.

'Dick!' Hilary put down her knitting and hurried into the
hall. 'Darling,' she cried as the door opened. 'How wonderful you're home so early—'

Her voice trailed away. The man already in the hall was
not Dick, but David Horner. She stared at him as he smiled

at her. Then her eyes dropped from his face to his gloved hands, and she felt weak with fear.

'Sorry to disappoint you,' he said, closing the flat's front door behind him. 'I doubt if your husband will be home for some time yet, and I want to speak to you first.'

'How—how did you get in?' she heard herself ask, as if the question mattered now.

'I used to keep an eye on the flat when the Porters were on holiday,' said Horner, 'so I've a spare key.'

'They forgot to mention it,' said Hilary, wondering how in these circumstances she could make such idiotic conversation.

'Let's go into the sitting-room, Hilary.'

'David, I'm—I'm busy. What do you want?'

'I told you. To talk.'

And afterwards? It was a question she didn't need to ask, she realized. But Dick will get you, she thought, sooner or later he'll get you.

Hilary had little hope of saving herself. She guessed that Horner had a gun in his pocket—probably the Smith & Wesson .38 with which he'd shot Gemma Fielding—and she kept her mind firmly away from garrottes and garrotting. She knew that, physically, with a baby inside her, she would be no match for him in spite of her training. Not that the baby would be saved whatever she could or couldn't do. The bastard would kill him—or her—too.

Involuntarily tears began to fill Hilary's eyes as she obeyed Horner's instructions and led the way into the sitting-room. She sat on the chair he pointed to, and turned off the television set. She told herself that her only hope was to keep him talking and pray for a miracle.

'What do you want to talk about, David?' she asked, surprised at the steadiness of her voice.

'I want you to tell me how much your old man, Detective Chief Inspector Tansey, really knows about these so-called

Marylebone murders. Much more than the public's been told, I bet.'

Hilary did her best to maintain the fiction that this was a friendly conversation. 'A certain amount,' she replied. 'And then, of course, there's what he merely suspects.'

'Such as?'

'That Gemma Fielding's murderer was someone who had once loved her, that in a way he still loved her. After all, she was an exciting woman, wasn't she?'

David Horner exploded. 'She was an arrogant bitch!' he cried. 'I saved her life and yet she wouldn't even give me a date. She pretended I'd done nothing. She preferred having it off with that fool Steve Cranworth.'

David Horner proceeded to give his version of Gemma's accident with her motorbike on the High Street. It bore little resemblance to the story Steve had told Tansey. According to Horner, he had dashed into the road and thrown Gemma off her bike just in time to rescue her from the wheels of a heavy lorry.

'At great risk to myself,' he said rather pompously. 'Great risk to myself,' he repeated as if the reiteration made the tale more credible. 'I might have been killed. But was she grateful? No!'

'And that's why you decided to kill her?' said Hilary gently after a moment's thought.

'When she took up with Steve Cranworth, yes. I used to follow her, though she didn't realize it, and I got to know a lot about her and the Cranworths—'

Horner stopped abruptly, his head cocked sideways as he listened. Hilary listened too, tense and straining. She had heard that sound again, the sound of a key in the lock. This time it had to be Dick, home early because she'd not been well, entering the flat unsuspectingly. For a moment she was overwhelmed—with relief for herself and fear for him.

Horner was already on his feet, the Smith & Wesson in his hand.

Chief Inspector Tansey walked into the room with seeming nonchalance. He threw one quick glance at Hilary and then, reassured that so far she was safe, regarded Horner calmly, taking no notice of the revolver. This wasn't the first time in his career that, unarmed, he had confronted a loaded gun, and from his point of view the situation was less unexpected than Hilary had assumed.

Racing up the stairs, Tansey had found Mrs Horner by his front door. Her eyes were red with weeping, her hair dishevelled and there was a weal across one cheek as if she had been struck. Never before had he seen the normally neat woman in such a state. She pointed wordlessly at his door.

Tansey realized this was no moment for more than a few words. He said simply, 'David's in there?'

She nodded. 'With his father's gun.'

'OK.' Tansey thought for a moment, and later was to wonder how he had managed to remain so calm and think so lucidly when Hilary was in such desperate danger.

'Go downstairs, Mrs Horner,' he said finally. 'There's a grey car outside. Tell the man—it's my Sergeant Sester— to send for back up—reinforcements—and an ambulance. He'll look after you. Hurry. Now!'

Tansey had forced himself to wait until Mrs Horner had gone down one flight of stairs before he had put his key in the lock. He hoped he could rely on her, though even a garbled message would alert Sester. Meanwhile, he must do his best to deal with the situation himself.

'Hello, David,' he said casually. 'What are you doing here?'

'As if you don't know, Chief Inspector. I always suspected you were cleverer than the papers said.'

'Give me the gun, David.' Tansey spoke soothingly.

'You're not going to shoot me. What would be the point?
It's always a bad idea to shoot a policeman. And, Hilary
—' he paused, keeping his voice level—'you go downstairs,
darling. Sester's there.'

As he spoke Tansey was moving slowly towards Horner,
his hand outstretched as if he were totally convinced that
Horner would obey him. Hilary stood up. She hesitated.
She didn't want to go—to leave Dick—

The decision was taken from her.

'No! Stay where you are!' shouted Horner. 'I'm going to
shoot. I'll kill you, both of you!'

He raised the revolver and fired point blank at Tansey.
The Chief Inspector, who had hardly dared to hope that
his ploy would work and had been prepared for sudden
action, leapt to one side and fell to the floor. But simultaneously Hilary flung herself between the two men. She
never felt the bullet enter her body.

It was three days before Hilary Tansey came out of intensive
care. She was still very weak, but she would live. She had
lost the baby.

Dick Tansey sat beside her hospital bed. The room was
full of flowers and cards sent by well-wishers, many from
the police, but some of them unexpected like the spray of
orchids from Harry and Steve Cranworth. There were even
some from the media, which was now full of praise for
Detective Chief Inspector Tansey.

Tansey held Hilary's hand in silence, aware that so far
they had had little opportunity to discuss the case.

At last Hilary said, 'Dick, tell me what happened. I
remember David lifting his gun. He was going to shoot you.
Then I woke up in hospital.'

'You saved my life, darling.'

This wasn't strictly true, though it was to become a family
myth. In fact, Tansey had anticipated Horner. He had

rolled away and was on his feet ready to tackle the man before he realized that Hilary had been shot. As Sester burst into the room, he was already wrestling the weapon out of Horner's hands.

Hilary said, 'How—'

'I knew you'd ask that,' answered Tansey. 'In a way, it all came together because of something Steve Cranworth told me on the phone. After all the red herrings and the false indications, it was he who brought home to me the suggestion that—'

Hilary interrupted him. '—that David Horner might meet all the criteria.'

'Exactly. And in fact, he did. Horner was one of the "Faithfuls". There was that episode in the High Street. He wanted Gemma, but Gemma had no time for him and had become Steve Cranworth's girlfriend instead, which provided a motive. He had the means and the facilities, including a motorbike licence. And by now the blood and tissue samples have put the matter beyond doubt. What made the case so damned difficult was his plan to hide the murder that mattered among other killings connected with the Cranworths.' Tansey looked at his wife doubtfully. 'Do you see what I mean?'

'Of course, Dick.'

'Anyway, I began to think that I should seriously consider David Horner as a suspect. On the chance that I was right I came home to our flat quickly—to get you away to safety before my inquiries could put you in danger.'

Hilary considered this for a moment, then clutched at his hand and said, 'What will happen to him?'

'He's made a full confession, and he'll be found guilty. There's no doubt of that. But I expect his counsel will try for "diminished responsibility"—he could use the fetish about laying out the bodies on the bed, for example. At any rate, whatever happens he'll be put away for a long time.

It's his mother I'm sorry for. She's collapsed and been admitted to a nursing home.'

'Poor dear!'

'Yes. It was thanks to her meeting me in the hall and doing what I told her that Sester was able to get the ambulance there so quickly. So in a sense she saved you, darling.'

'But not our baby.'

'No, but the doctor says there's no reason why we shouldn't try again, once you're strong enough.'

'Of course we will,' said Hilary. 'And Sester can be a godfather.'